D1740289

Firebrands

Firebrands

A NOVEL

MARC MÉNARD

Translated by **PETER McCAMBRIDGE**

Original version published in French as *Brasiers* by Les Éditions Somme, 2021.
Copyright © 2021 by Marc Ménard, Tête première.
Copyright © 2022 by Peter McCambridge for the English translation.

All rights reserved. No part of this book may be reproduced, for any reason or by any means, without permission in writing from the publisher.

Copyediting: Jennifer McMorran
Author photo: Claude Barbeau
Cover image: Greg Rakozy (Unsplash)
Cover design: Leila Marshy, Debbie Geltner
Book design: DiTech

Library and Archives Canada Cataloguing in Publication

Title: Firebrands : a novel / Marc Ménard ; translated from the French by Peter McCambridge.
Other titles: Brasiers. English
Names: Ménard, Marc, 1960- author. | McCambridge, Peter, 1979- translator.
Description: Translation of: Brasiers.
Identifiers: Canadiana (print) 20210335890 | Canadiana (ebook) 20210335904 | ISBN 9781773901053 (softcover) | ISBN 9781773901060 (EPUB) | ISBN 9781773901077 (PDF)
Classification: LCC PS8576.E534 B7313 2022 | DDC C843/.6—dc23

Printed and bound in Canada

Legal deposit – Library and Archives Canada and Bibliothèque et Archives nationales du Québec, 2022

The publisher gratefully acknowledges the support of the Government of Canada through the Canada Council for the Arts and the Canada Book Fund. We acknowledge the financial support of the Government of Canada through the National Translation Program for Book Publishing, an initiative of the Action Plan for Official Languages – 2018-2023: Investing in Our Future, for our translation activities.

We are grateful to the Government of Quebec through the Société du développement culturel and the Programme de credit d'impôt pour l'édition de livres—Gestion SODEC.

Linda Leith Publishing
Montreal
www.lindaleith.com

"Most people deceive themselves with a pair of faiths: they believe in *eternal memory* (of people, things, deeds, nations) and in *redressability* (of deeds, mistakes, sins, wrongs). Both are false faiths. In reality the opposite is true: everything will be forgotten and nothing will be redressed."

Milan Kundera
The Joke

"The world is a cancer eating itself away."

Henry Miller
Tropic of Cancer

Chapter 1

Montreal, October 2002

Two days from now, Philippe thought, I'll be 40.

He'd dreaded it for the longest time. The date had always seemed so permanent, so definitive. Like the summit of a mountain you'd looked at your whole life, a far-off destination you knew was inevitable but were still in no rush to get to. And once you reached the top, if your ticket was still good, you only got to go down the other side, following the twists and turns of a path long like a tired snake, lower and lower.

Philippe's still-thick hair was barely starting to be flecked by white. His abdomen had a give to it that, 20 years earlier, his flat, hard stomach hadn't known, but he hadn't yet resorted to hiding it under shapeless sweaters. He hadn't smoked in more than a year, kept his drinking reasonable, jogged three times a week, and regularly hit the weights. But there was no getting around it: in two days, he'd be 40.

He sighed.

The young boy at his side looked up and held out his hand with a smile. Philippe took the little hand in his and gave it a squeeze. The light turned green, and they crossed the street. Once they were in the schoolyard, Philippe squatted down next to his son Dominic. In under two minutes, the bell would ring and the children would line up outside the door. He looked around for Lucas, his older son, among the crowd of kids as they shouted and ran around. He found him pretty much right away, hanging from the monkey bars, feet dangling into the void. Their eyes met briefly, and he flashed him a furtive smile that Lucas returned just as discreetly. He was barely ten, Philippe thought, and Lucas was already distancing himself, as though ashamed at the thought his friends might catch him smiling over at his dad.

Philippe turned back to his younger son, fixed the collar on his windbreaker, and planted a noisy kiss on his cheek. Dominic gave him a smile that alone made the trip worth it. Philippe stood back up and watched with his hands in his pockets as his son walked off, backpack and lunchbox slung over his shoulder, swaying beneath the load. The bell rang. The shouts around him grew louder, and the children began to converge on the school. Philippe sighed again and began the walk back home.

The Friday morning was cool for October. The sky was a blindingly clear azure, a sure sign of the last throes of summer. As always, the heavy traffic had ground to an impatient standstill on Henri-Bourassa. He crossed the boulevard, and the blare of the traffic quickly faded, replaced by the leaves rustling in the wind, the warbling of the starlings, and the squirrels scampering through the maples. The canopy formed by the double row of trees made for a protective screen that more often than not left Philippe feeling calm and collected.

But not today. Today the canopy was gloomy and left him with the same suffocating sensation as the too-low ceiling of a damp cave, the walls of the houses around him cold and smooth as death row. He made a face as he neared home, depressed at the thought of starting his workday. Especially since what was waiting on his desk was a long-winded, sleep-inducing treatise on the perils of globalization, which he was to read and report on for the small publishing house he regularly freelanced for. Almost 40 and still having to take on contracts like that to put bread on the table—he couldn't take it anymore.

If that was going to be his state of mind, it was shaping up to be a long day.

Maybe he'd take the day off, he thought to himself. He'd put his feet up with a steaming-hot coffee and a good book. An afternoon nap. A dry martini at five o'clock. And that would be that.

His house was in sight. He buried his chin down into his coat collar and quickened his pace. A car he didn't know was parked outside his house, an old Toyota Corolla painted a faded burgundy. He barely gave it a glance before cutting across the paved surface of his parking spot, climbing the few steps that led to his balcony, his key already out. He heard a car door open then close behind him.

"Philippe!"

He was stopped in his tracks. He knew that voice. He hadn't heard it in 15 years, but there was no doubt about it. Low and gravelly, with something vaguely Germanic about it. A voice that had always radiated, the way he remembered it, uncommon strength and assurance. Though at that very moment, even when uttering no more than the two syllables of his first name, the voice seemed weak and indecisive, more hoarse than husky, weary.

"Mora?" he said, whirling around.

Standing in the road, both hands on the roof of his car, Robert Moranowitz gave Philippe a nod and a tired smile. Philippe plodded over to the Corolla, distraught at how Mora looked. His features were the picture of exhaustion: hollowed-out cheeks, and eyelids drooping down like crumpled curtains over washed-out grey eyes. His hair was dull and greasy, grey in places, and his shoulders were hunched, his back threatening to give way beneath a seemingly unbearable weight. The raincoat he was wearing was loose-fitting, but he still looked worryingly thin. A corpse, thought Philippe.

Philippe hesitated between tears and anger, not sure if he should be happy or furious. He wanted to cry with joy, to give Mora a kiss and hold him in his arms tight enough to crack a few bones, then strangle him and beat him black and blue for his unbroken silence, for 15 years without a word. But sadness won the day; the powerful, indestructible man he'd once known now resembled no more than a shadow of his former self.

Seeing Philippe's face fall, Mora shrugged his shoulders, putting on a wry smile.

"I look like a ghost, eh? Better yet: the reincarnation of my grandfather, if he'd made it out of the death camps!" he added, raising his arms to the heavens. "The truth is, alas, much more unremarkable."

Mora shrugged his shoulders again, and Philippe didn't know what to say.

"Hepatitis C," Mora told him. "My liver's toast, and all the meds I'm on are chipping away at the rest."

His laugh rolled around in his throat like a pebble on a riverbed. Philippe took a step forward, and their hands clasped over the roof of the car. They stood like that for a moment, not saying a word.

"You coming in for a coffee?" Philippe asked.

"No, no. I want to have a chat, but not here. There must be a nice café around here somewhere."

Philippe ordered a latte and Mora a tea. Seeing Mora shiver and adjust the collar of his raincoat around his neck, Philippe suggested a table that was well away from the door. They sat opposite each other and, looking around them, stirred their drinks with the end of their spoons, like two painfully shy men who didn't know how to strike up a conversation.

Philippe rubbed his temples. He'd waited for a sign from Mora for a long time, hoping to see him reappear. A visit, a phone call, a letter, an email, anything. As the years passed, he'd had to come to terms with the incredible idea that Mora wasn't invincible. That he'd finally gone one step too far. He'd crossed the line and paid the price. Confronted with silence, Philippe had tried hard to forget Mora, his plans, his friends, and his network. Mora and the harebrained schemes he'd allowed himself to be dragged into.

But how could he forget? How could he erase from his memory the intense discussions, the laughter and the tears, the cause he had believed in, the flawed reasoning and the false pretences, not to mention all the violence they'd waded into?

Until that morning, Philippe had thought he'd managed it. At the very least, he thought he'd buried the young Philippe, the hothead with the devil-may-care attitude. But he was realizing that his friend's unexpected reappearance was reawakening old demons, the angry young man who was ready to support Mora's struggle.

The bitterness that washed over him was so strong he couldn't hold back a grimace. Mora replied with a smile that briefly revived the memory of past vigour. He straightened his tall body and brought his hands together above his cup of tea.

"I know you can't wait to give me the third degree, but just hold off a minute, would you? First, I'd like to talk about you. I've been doing my homework."

Philippe raised his eyebrows in concern. Mora "doing his homework" on someone was no joke.

Mora gave Philippe a look and plunged his hand into the inside pocket of his raincoat, producing a bundle of paper. He unfolded the sheets and carefully smoothed them out.

"What do we have here?" Mora went on, setting a pair of reading glasses down onto his nose. "Let's start in 1987, if that's okay with you. June 1987, to be more precise. You've rushed back from Paris, PhD abandoned, no great surprise considering how little work you put into it. In Montreal, you get back in touch with a few professors you used to work with, who find you a contract or two as a research assistant, enough to get you back on your feet. You forget all about macroeconomics and the world economy to study media and culture, even going so far as to start a PhD in sociology, but only for a year. You seem to have a recurring problem with PhDs, by the look of things. Unless you just run out of steam?"

"Drop it."

"Fair enough. In the meantime, you try to get back with Madeleine, who's been back in Montreal since Christmas 1986. Congratulations. I never realized you were so determined to follow your heart."

Philippe shook his head, but Mora didn't even look up.

"It worked out, and you've been living together since winter 1988. Madeleine works in radio as a freelance researcher until she carves out a place for herself. Meanwhile, you hop from contract to contract, researching for government ministries and various professional associations. You too end up making a name for yourself, and slowly but surely you become one of the go-to guys in your field."

"I'm not sure that's how I'd have put it."

"Doesn't matter. In 1993, you have a little boy, Lucas. Then a second in 1996, Dominic. Unfortunately, that same year your father dies, then your mother one year later. The inheritance isn't a fortune, but since you're an only son it's enough of a little nest egg to substantially improve things for your family, and you buy a house in Ahuntsic. All good so far?"

"More or less, yeah."

"Great. So let's move on to the other side of your life. Just give me a sec."

Mora peered down at his pile of paper.

"Here we go! You belong to groups that support the poor, immigrants, the elderly, and the homeless. Under-the-radar pressure groups concerned with protecting the environment, sustainable development, GMOs, and the impact of globalization. It's a long list and, to be honest, anyone would be doing well to join the dots between them all. If you ask me, it looks a lot like you're spreading yourself in all directions, looking in vain for the one cause to make everything make sense. Ah yes, and the best is still to come."

"What?"

"You're also a coach's assistant with Lucas's baseball team, Mosquito category. Shame the season's over, I'd have loved to see you at work. Just imagining you in your uniform makes me shudder."

"Very funny."

"Thing is, if it weren't for the small matter of a file that's still open at the Canadian Security Intelligence Service…"

Philippe almost choked.

"What? CSIS has a file on me?"

"Of course, they do. What did you think? They're paid to open files and gather information on people who pose a threat to this wonderful country of ours. But don't worry: there's nothing serious. Just a lot of old stuff everyone's forgotten about by now. Almost nothing really. Wait, just let me check something…"

Mora began leafing frantically through his pile of paper, while Philippe rubbed his temples again.

"There we are!" Mora rejoiced, brandishing a particularly crumpled page. "Member of the Montreal Citizens' Group and the pressure group For a Renewed Socialism… helping squatters who are demanding social housing and feminist shock troops… protests… the odd fight… accusations of assault, twice… vandalism… Nothing serious, like I said."

"Good."

Despite trying his best to appear unmoved, Philippe was a little relieved.

"Now what's really surprising about your file is that there's nothing after 1986. I have no choice but to conclude that you've been transformed into an upstanding family man. Your conscience is clear: taking care of the kids, volunteering for respectable groups, and no doubt mowing your lawn once a week."

"It's a bit depressing, when you put it like that."

"That it is. Did I forget anything?"

"You did. Why is this middle-class existence of any interest to you? And, while I'm at it: where the hell were you for the past 15 years, and why didn't you ever let me know you were still alive, you bastard?"

Mora dropped his act and turned serious again.

"Why? For one very simple reason: I managed to find a way out. But since I could already hear the police sirens, I didn't try to catch up to you. I ran away instead."

"And Wolf?"

Mora leaned over the table and clasped his hands together.

"Can you believe that after all those years, he ended up getting caught. The bullet I left in his leg must've slowed him down."

"Why didn't you try to get in touch with me?"

"Because you'd have wanted to meet up. Wolf might have been in prison, but his men might have been looking for us. It was better to go our separate ways, for both our sakes. By the time I was sure the danger had passed, you were already back in Montreal. I decided to leave things as they were. I'd had enough of dragging you into everything. I'd screwed things up for you enough as it was. I'd rather let you think I was dead. It seemed easier that way."

"And the others? What happened to them? I couldn't get in touch with anyone at all."

"They did what I told them to do if things went south: cut off all contact, move home, forget the whole sorry business, and start over."

"And why was I never told that?"

Mora chuckled. He straightened up in his seat and crossed his arms.

"No need. You followed it all to the letter. Out of instinct. Just like I knew you would."

"Thanks for the vote of confidence, but it would've been nice to hear it, all the same."

Mora shrugged, and the two of them went quiet again.

"And why the sudden urge to see me again?" Philippe asked, a terrible feeling gnawing at his stomach.

Mora's eyes suddenly lit up with a feverish glow.

"Wolf was freed a year ago. He's rebuilt everything, member by member, cell by cell. Working out of the shadows, as usual. It took me a year, but I managed to track him down. It's payback time, Philippe. Time to root out the weeds, once and for all."

Philippe raised his eyebrows in disbelief, waiting for Mora to go on.

"But I'll need your help."

"That's what I was afraid of," Philippe replied, his voice deathly quiet.

Chapter 2

Montreal, September 1986

Philippe was an angry young man.

His mother had often told him as much. "You always were. You were angry from the moment you were born. It was otherworldly, anger of Olympic proportions. You'd shout and scream so hard at daycare, people were worried the other babies would vanish into thin air. And you'd keep on wailing like a boat siren, like you were calling out the world for all its injustices. Only a few days old, and you were already up in arms."

Almost a teenager, Philippe still hadn't calmed down any, and was beginning to see that his mother wasn't so much against his moaning and groaning as against how he rejected the established order, his refusal to submit to the rules. "Can't you just fall in line like everyone else?" each of her sighs seemed to say.

Why should he "fall in line"? Why should he accept the indefensible and remain unmoved by injustice? He never did find an answer to those questions.

His father might have been able to calm him down a little, but he had fallen in line to the point of disappearing. He avoided all discussion and left the room at the slightest hint of an argument, leaving discipline to his wife. Who sighed all the harder.

The anger that brewed inside Philippe was fuelled by his father's languid torpor and his mother's conformism, and it grew steadily over the years. He left the family nest when he was 18. There was no wailing and gnashing of teeth, only the firm belief that he had the courage of his convictions: how could anyone hope to change the world when they still lived at home with their parents?

"Changing the world" was what he wanted to do with his life. He became an activist, someone for whom political commitment had to take the form of direct action. But this didn't bring him any satisfaction: no matter how hard he tried, the world stayed just as it was.

This inability to "change the world" became Philippe's greatest source of frustration. Every day he'd repeat his intention to himself like a mantra. What times he lived in! Just reading the newspaper was enough to send him into a rage. The absurd injustices of the world only grew on him: the poverty and the unemployment, the inequalities, the iniquities, the abuses and acts of violence of all kinds that leapt off the page at him like grenades. His rage grew by the day, and his sense of powerlessness with it. Everything he tried flopped. He discussed and argued, tried to change minds. Wrote in newspapers and magazines. Demonstrated, protested, vandalized. Walked with a swagger and threw punches. With no results to speak of. Nothing at all, just a ton of people who gave him strange looks, the looks reserved for those who are out of their minds.

Despite his frustration, an irresistible urge to do something stayed with him. To kick out at all the exploiters, strangle them, make mincemeat out of them. Better still: to blow up their sumptuous homes and shiny new cars, to blast the idiots' assurance into smithereens as they pickled in their repugnant individualism.

By the end of the day, Philippe's anger would have petered out, drained by its own futility. There was only one thing for it. To turn his back on the swamp, get out of there, and start over somewhere new. From scratch. He wouldn't be leaving much behind anyway: parents who didn't understand him, a relationship that wasn't much of anything anymore, a few friends here and there. He had to admit that as the years had gone by, helped by his fury and frustration, he'd managed to drive everyone away. Now he was all alone in a desert of his own making, with no emotional ties to speak of.

With a master's in economics under his belt, he'd come to a fork in the road when he turned 24. Either he followed the implacable logic of his initial thinking and took off in search of a better future, or he settled down and found himself a sensible job to pay off his student debt.

He didn't hesitate for long. The fleeting vision of a soul-destroying job in a bank, or working in insurance—or, worse still, for a brokerage company—made up his mind.

He had nothing to lose by starting over. Nothing to lose and everything to gain.

He was off.

But where to?

France slowly began to seem like a possibility.

Since François Mitterrand's socialist government had come to power, the age-old fantasy of France as a refuge for Quebec intellectuals thirsting for freedom was back in vogue. Philippe, of course, was aware that after a short spell marked by a handful of social measures and head-turning nationalizations, the Mitterrand government had also followed policies more typical of the right. Although he preferred a loudmouth but realistic left to a smug and condescending right.

And then the elections of spring 1986 had seen Jean-Marie Le Pen's National Front burst into the Assemblée nationale with 9.7% of the vote. Things were shaping up as though ideologies, once again, were grouping around either end of the spectrum: left and right were ready to clash. Philippe was determined to be right there when it happened, to be watching from the front row.

He got himself a study grant and signed up for a PhD in economics at the University of Paris VIII in Saint-Denis. Thinking he was being clever, he managed to combine his PhD with a France-Quebec exchange program, which would land him another source of income for three months as well as an apartment.

Letting someone else find him a place to live seemed like a good idea at the time. That was his first mistake.

Chapter 3

Montreal, October 2002

Elbows resting on the kitchen table, his chin propped up by his hands, Philippe stared into his coffee. A scrap of paper on which Mora had scribbled his phone number lay between him and the cup.

He should have told him there was just no way. It wasn't a complicated word: "No." He cursed his cowardice, the phony tact that had made him agree to "think about it." There was no point thinking about it. He'd made up his mind: there was not a chance he was going with Mora.

He eyed the phone that seemed to be taunting him. Philippe swore and told himself he was a fool.

Even if he did agree to go with Mora, he knew he no longer had what it took. The all-consuming rage, the flame that had to be burning to take you to the brink—all he had now was a pile of ash that had been swept into a closet reserved for bad memories. "We're nothing without anger," Mora used to say. Philippe could still feel that anger. Nothing was easier than flying off the handle. He only had to open a newspaper or turn on the news. But now it took more than anger to get him to take action.

The problem was that he no longer believed in the need to "root out the weeds." He was happy to leave that to people younger than he was. Time had taken its toll on him, like it does on everyone. Mora had been right about that. He was nothing more than a father about to turn 40 who volunteered for a few good causes and seldom thought of anything other than the demands of family life.

So that was that. All he had to do was pick up the damned phone and set him straight.

But he didn't budge from his chair, and he felt less calm than ever. This is ridiculous, he thought. If he couldn't bring himself to say no to Mora, it was because he didn't want to let him down. To lose his friend all over again, this time for good.

He wondered at his reasoning for a moment, but he had to admit he'd been lying to himself. It wasn't about letting Mora down. Mora reappearing had made him realize just how long his own life had been bland and on hold. He was about to turn 40, and the truth was that, aside from bringing up two kids, writing the odd quickly forgotten article or two, honouring contracts that were of no importance, and making his wife more or less happy (even then, you'd have to ask her), he hadn't done a thing with his life. He felt useless, unneeded. A big bag of hot air.

The adrenalin coursing through his veins. Feeling light-headed, like he was living his life at 100 miles an hour. That's what he missed. The feeling that he was taking part in something that mattered, that he had an influence on the world around him. When had he last felt like that? When Dominic had fallen down the stairs the week before, scraping his knee and crying his heart out, his head buried in his dad's shoulder? Or when Lucas had pitched three perfect innings for his baseball team? No, the emotions he was missing were much more visceral than that.

Another glance told him the phone was still taunting him, stoic and unruffled though it was.

What was Mora proposing exactly? He didn't have the faintest idea. Mora hadn't given any details, content to dangle the bait in front of his nose. A big juicy worm named

Hans Wolf. There would have been no point pressing him, Mora wouldn't have said another word. Mora the Master Manipulator.

Mora was a team player. He no doubt had a few buddies by his side, a whole network straining to reach the same goal: catch Wolf and get him to pay his debts. All of them. It was tempting.

Philippe's resolve wavered. He felt a shiver run along the length of his spine, like an itch in his muscles, a need to stand up and get down to business. It was awake now, the thing that had been resting inside him, dozing at his very core for far too long now. The rumblings of a volcano that was coming to life after years of lying dormant, suddenly ready to explode, fuelled by the thought of progressing towards a goal, of finally doing something. Although Mora's plan, whatever it was, could only end in disaster, Philippe felt the excitement spread through his body like a powerful drug.

Worst of all, he knew that Mora was in no doubt that Philippe would say yes. His face had lit up when he'd handed him that damned piece of paper. It was like he'd never known anything else than following Mora. He'd already sold his soul to him. To Mora the Charmer.

No, no, no. He was no longer young and brainless. He was 40 years old. He had a job, a wife, and two children.

Without giving the phone so much as another glance, Philippe stood up and strode towards the kitchen counter, ready to make himself another coffee. He stopped when he was halfway there. He looked at his watch, swivelled around, took two steps, and opened the freezer, reaching for the bottle of vodka. A good old dry martini. That's what he needed. A double, well shaken. Shaken, not stirred. And Mora could go to hell.

Chapter 4

Paris, September 1986

As excited as a schoolboy, Philippe found himself in Paris. But a strange ball welled up in his throat, a hint of the anxiety that threatened to overwhelm him. Why on earth did he feel so anxious? He knew Paris, after all, he told himself. He'd spent seven days there as a tourist, rushing from one attraction to the next, three years earlier.

He immediately realized how ridiculous that thought had been: seven days was nothing compared to the three or four years he was getting ready to spend there.

With the Gare du Nord at its busiest, he cleared a path through the crowd, weighed down by his backpack and two suitcases crammed full of books and papers. After elbowing his way through, he managed to find a seat.

The trip was taking forever, and the scenery that passed by on the other side of the window was nothing short of dismal. The room that the people organizing his internship had found for him was in Sarcelles, a suburb far to the north of Paris. The schlep from the train station to his apartment gave him a fair idea of his surroundings: it was one of the suburbs that had gone up in a hurry after the war, a solution to the housing crisis and now home to every ethnic group in the world.

When he'd reached his destination, Philippe dragged his bags and the rest of himself inside. The stairwells and hallway were dirty and dusty. In the showers just opposite his room, the water flowed nonstop, like a public fountain. Lots of doors were open, and people filed from one room to the next, making a constant racket. The building smelled of merguez and chicken in peanut sauce, of cilantro, cumin, saffron, and cloves. The very place to write a doctoral thesis, he thought to himself wryly.

At last he went into his room. He closed the door behind him, threw his bags on the bed, and had a look around. The room was tiny. A bed, a bookcase, a small wooden table, two chairs, a bedside lamp, and a sink.

He collapsed onto a chair. One of the legs gave way under his weight. He tried again with a second chair, which this time was up to the task. He sighed, fished the pack of Gauloises Blondes out of his shirt pocket, and lit a cigarette with a trembling hand. Blowing the smoke out between his lips, he noticed a bug making its way over to him, spryly zigzagging its way across the floor. Just as the cockroach was about to scurry between his legs, he brought his heel down on it hard, and lifted his foot to stare at the crushed insect, its body writhing pathetically.

He took a puff of the cigarette and resolved to find himself somewhere else to live.

Laurent Besson. A French guy he'd met at a lecture on globalization given by Philippe's thesis supervisor. Laurent was from ClermontFerrand and, just like Philippe, had come to Paris to do a PhD in political economy at the University of Paris VIII in Saint-Denis. Laurent asked him if he'd like to go for a beer, and Philippe was only too happy to accept.

Laurent took him to a café on Boulevard Saint-Germain that was far enough from Boulevard Saint-Michel not to be overrun with tourists. The café's long glass façade looked out over a corner, and they walked in through the wide-open door-cum-window. "This café is where my friends and I hang out," Laurent told him as he raised a hand for the server. "We come here almost every day."

Philippe and Laurent talked and talked as they knocked back one beer after the next. They talked about their theses, their favourite authors, about Quebec and France, about the political situation in each country, about how young people had no future ahead of them, about all paths being blocked, there being no way out, about economic inequalities, the homeless, the ambient racism, the rise of the National Front, and, of course, the never-ending wave of terrorist attacks that had plunged France into a state of paranoia and hysteria, opening the door to a heavy-handed reaction by the police. A discussion that came naturally in a cozy café. Others joined them as the hours passed.

Thomas was the first to appear, a psychology student from Berlin. Followed by Meredith, Olivier, Marie, Maurice, Heinrich, Liset… Philippe was practically hyperventilating. The evening was taking on a dimension far beyond his wildest dreams; it was as though he was at an international meeting of young, fun-seeking, left-leaning intellectuals. It was an incredible breath of fresh air. Everyone spoke at once, laughter erupted from all sides, and the beer kept coming. The discussions veered towards English, then came back to French, before turning to German. The conversation was chaotic, warm, and joyful. Philippe was slowly giving himself over to a happy drunkenness when she came in.

Madeleine. She'd come over from Montreal for a three-month internship in Paris. Her face was a perfect oval, her brown hair was shoulder-length, and, behind her steel-rimmed glasses, her deep green eyes sparkled with intelligence. She sat next to Philippe, innocently asking what brought him to Paris. Not content with the concise answer that tends to follow such a question, Philippe launched into a convoluted explanation of his studies, an interminable monologue on the history of economic thought over the course of the twentieth century. She listened religiously, occasionally asking a question or two that would send Philippe off on new tangents. He knew that he was getting himself in a muddle, but he kept on talking. He was chaos itself, his mouth spewing forth a stream of words that sought to cover up the feelings that had suddenly come over him. He could see surprise and curiosity in Madeleine's eyes, perhaps even something approaching interest in the face of so much intensity and passion, and so he didn't trust himself to stop talking, fearful of breaking the spell. Just as he thought he had run out of things to say, that he might drop with exhaustion, she picked up where he had left off, telling him all about her political science studies, what had brought her to Paris, her eagerness to discover new horizons, to leave dull and dreary Montreal behind.

He paid absolutely no heed to anything she said about her partner waiting for her in Montreal. He inched closer as she spoke, their two bodies forming a protective cocoon against the hubbub around them. They brushed hands, their thighs touched. Philippe stroked her hair, took in the delicious aroma of her neck, enjoyed the rapturous softness of her earlobe against his lip. She didn't rebuff his advances; he sensed that she was like a flower ready to open at his touch.

Suddenly she looked down at her watch and leapt to her feet. She leaned in towards him, mumbled a few words of apology, then planted a noisy kiss full on his lips.

She hurried outside, leaving Philippe speechless, both won over and desperate.

Chapter 5

Montreal, October 2002

The noise was deafening. A forge clawed at his ears, its breath scalding his neck. Dazed, he opened his eyes and closed them again, trying to gather his wits. It was night. Glowing red lights danced at the windows of the building across the street. He was slumped in a pile of debris, his sweater snagged against a rough brick wall. He looked up to see a long, open window from which there emerged a thick plume of black smoke.

A dull thud sounded behind him, a powerful explosion followed by the crystal-clear tinkle of shattering glass. A hail of shards rained down onto him, a shower of burning confetti. The window above him was gone, blown out by the explosion. A tongue of fire slipped through the opening and licked at the brick wall, towering high into the sky as it gave off acrid smoke that reeked of gasoline and melted rubber. A look of panic crossed his face as he struggled to stand up. He put his weight on his left arm, but pain shot through his shoulder. He dropped back to the ground. Slivers of glass bit into his cheek. The heat was infernal. The smoke thickened around him, and he began to choke. He rubbed his eyelids, coughed hard enough to bring up a lung, and in one despairing effort tried to pick himself back up, taking care to protect his left arm. Amid the rubble, he managed to bring himself to his knees. He felt a warm, sticky liquid on his hands. They were covered with blood.

Philippe awoke with a start, out of breath and covered in sweat. Everything was calm around him. All he could hear was the shrill whistle of his own breath. Instinctively, he put his hands up, noting with relief that they were dry and white.

It had been years since he'd had that nightmare. A nightmare that had tormented him for the longest time, night after night, like Chinese water torture. Then the hellish nights had become less frequent, until after a year or two he'd regained the restful sleep of a man with a clear conscience. Until that night.

He rubbed hard at his face and rolled over to his left. The covers had been pushed back, freeing the sheets. Madeleine was no longer at his side. He sighed and tried to put his thoughts in order.

Late that afternoon, Philippe had gone to pick up the children from school. Then, eager to bring an end to a week that just wouldn't end, he'd rented a movie and ordered a pizza. The kids had eaten their pizza, watched their movie, then gone to bed—far too early, if you asked them, of course. Then he and Madeleine had seen out the rest of the evening with a good Madiran. They'd chatted about this and that, mostly the kids. Then they'd gone upstairs to bed, each with a book. Philippe had quickly set his down and turned off the bedside lamp. He'd stretched out on his belly, his head buried in the pillow, then shamelessly allowed his thigh to wander towards Madeleine's. He'd shifted his leg, quietly and with no sign of intent, as though trying to find a more comfortable position in which to fall asleep, each time allowing his skin to brush again hers. Moments later, he wrapped his thigh around Madeleine's, and she replied by lifting her leg slightly, leaving Philippe's knee resting against her pubic hair. He slid his hand down towards her abdomen, bringing his hand against the warmth of her round belly. Madeleine closed her book, put down her glasses, and turned to him. They made love.

It wasn't until they were almost asleep, the lights off, that Philippe finally found the courage to speak.

"Mora's alive. I saw him today."

The feeling of stabbing someone in the back was stronger than he had ever known.

"I've no choice," Philippe began, awkwardly.

Madeleine was sitting across from him, wrapped up tightly in her robe. She reached for his cigarettes. Smoke was spiralling around her in no time, a protective screen.

"We always have a choice," she snapped.

"No, Madeleine, not always. I thought it was over, too. It's not. I can't do anything about it. It has to end. We can't just pretend it's not happening."

"It's 'we' now, I hear. Interesting. Is it you talking, or is it Mora?"

"Dammit, Madeleine, would you just listen? We've been through it before. You know we have. It's happening again: nobody bothers with people like Wolf. It's like all the far-right crazies just disappeared. That hasn't happened. You know it, and I know it. They're still spouting the same knuckle-dragging ideas as before, they're still plotting the same things. No one's paying any attention, and no one will take any interest until they strike again. And then it'll be too late."

Madeleine crushed her barely started cigarette in the ashtray.

"It sounded good coming from you when you were 25, Philippe. You're turning 40 now."

Philippe sighed with resignation.

"Sure, I get it. But I've been playing it out in my head for hours, and there's no two ways about it: I have no choice. If I don't do anything, every time I open the newspaper and read about an attack, I'll feel responsible. I'll be asking myself if I couldn't have prevented innocent people dying. I have no choice. I need to do something."

"Even if it costs you your life? Even if it means making me a widow and leaving your children orphans? Those people are sick, Philippe. They're crazy. They have no respect for human life. Do I really need to remind you?"

"I know, Madeleine. I know that. But we're not talking about organizing a suicide mission. We'll go just there, follow Wolf from a distance, then call the police. That's it! I owe Mora at least that."

Madeleine rolled her eyes and ran an angry hand through her hair.

"You don't owe him a thing! After how he manipulated you, then ignored you for 15 years, he's the one who owes you. He should leave you alone! That's what he owes you."

"You're going too far. He didn't manipulate me. I knew what I was doing back then. That's on me."

"And you really think things will be different today? Do you think they'll be any simpler? It wouldn't be the first time things didn't go according to plan with Mora."

"I'll make sure things stay simple. We won't even get close to them. We'll keep our distance, see what they're up to, then get out of there. Two days, three days tops, and it'll be over, I swear."

Madeleine stared hard at him, as though daring him. Philippe glowered back at her, but didn't say another word. Angrily, she lit another cigarette.

"Is that really the only thinking behind your decision, the people who might die? There wouldn't be anything else behind it, by any chance?"

"Like what?" Philippe frowned.

"Like revenge, for instance?"

He shrugged.

"That might be part of it. But it doesn't change anything, at the end of the day."

"No, that changes everything. When you're out for revenge, all rational thoughts go out the window. It twists your judgment, you can't tell right from wrong anymore. It makes you become like them. Is that really what you want? To become like them? Is that how you want your kids to see you? A man who was all out for revenge? Jesus, Philippe, can't you just let it go? Or let someone else go after those people?"

"Some things can't be wiped away, Madeleine. Some things can't be forgotten, let alone forgiven. I'm sorry. And as for letting someone else take care of them, don't make me laugh! No one gives a damn about those people. That's just the problem."

The silence hung in the air between them, thick and heavy. After a moment or two, Madeleine stubbed out her cigarette and stood up. Her whole body was shaking. She screamed with rage then stomped off into the bedroom.

Chapter 6

Paris, October 1986

Philippe settled into an unrelenting routine. Back and forth between Sarcelles, Saint-Denis, and Paris. Lectures at Paris VIII. Never-ending afternoons at the political studies library spent poring over books and papers, making photocopies, and taking notes. Round about six o'clock, he would invariably stuff his papers into his bag and walk along Boulevard Saint-Germain, mixing with the dense crowd until he reached the café where he'd meet up with his new friends. After something to eat, a beer, and a discussion or two, he would head home alone, taking the train north until he reached his far-off gloomy suburb and his miserable room.

He hadn't seen Madeleine again. She hadn't been back to the café.

He'd asked Laurent, who'd told him he didn't know her, knew nothing about her. Not a day went by without Philippe thinking of her, a golden opportunity he'd let slip through his fingers.

He felt so alone. A few hours spent fraternizing with his new friends proved a momentary distraction, but as soon as he was back in his room, besieged by smells from every corner of the world, that empty feeling took hold of him again. Surrounded by young workers who had just immigrated to the country, he could never manage to reach out to them or find anything in common. He was an outsider among the outsiders. Alone with his thoughts, which constantly drifted back to Madeleine.

On nights he couldn't sleep, he would get out of bed, pull back the drapes, open the window, and scan his suburb's lunar landscape. He'd light a cigarette and pour himself a glass of brandy. He'd have a think. Tell himself he was drinking and smoking too much. That he wasn't working hard enough, that his thesis was going nowhere. That his stay in Paris was slowly turning into a disaster. Late at night, in the relative silence that reigned at last, he would go back to bed, his head spinning and his throat raw, tumbling into a deep sleep as though falling into a bottomless well.

The sun had been hiding behind thick clouds for days, and a fine rain cut straight to the bone. Philippe walked through the café's picture windows looking like death warmed over. Although it was early, Laurent was there already, sitting at his table at the back of the glass corner and reading *Le Monde*. He looked up when Philippe's shadow fell over the newspaper and winced when he saw his haggard look.

"You look terrible. Is Sarcelles really that depressing?"

Philippe collapsed down beside him and waved a hand in the server's direction.

"Sarcelles is gonna be the death of me, no doubt about it. It's eating me alive, and it feels like I spend half my day on the train."

Laurent looked hard at him while he scratched his beard.

"I might have the answer for you…" he began.

"I'm listening," Philippe replied, suddenly interested.

"I know someone who's just come over from Montreal. He's been crashing with friends, but I know for a fact he just found an apartment he's looking to share."

"Really!"

Laurent was quick to dampen Philippe's enthusiasm.

"Now don't get carried away! He's not the easiest to get along with. Chances are, you won't hit it off at all. Do you want me to introduce you, all the same?"

Less than 30 minutes later, they were both at the Maison du Canada student housing centre, knocking at the door to a room at the far end of a long hallway.

They waited for a good two minutes, then the door opened to reveal a completely naked man. He was very tall, slender despite his broad shoulders, with an impressive set of pecs and tight, compact abs. His face was crumpled and his hair, disheveled. He rubbed at his eyes, before glaring at Laurent and Philippe. The blinds were closed, plunging the room into darkness. Even from the doorway, the room smelled unmistakably of sex. A naked woman was lying on the bed, which faced the door. She mumbled something, before burying herself under the covers.

"Robert!" Laurent greeted him, trying hard to sound cheerful. "Sorry to bother you. Do you have a couple of minutes?"

"What is it?"

"This is Philippe. I told you about him, remember? He's the Canadian who lives in the middle of nowhere, in Sarcelles. He'd be down for sharing your apartment."

Robert gave Philippe his full attention as he scratched his crotch.

"It's an F2. We'd call it a three-and-a-half back home. It's not the best, but it's clean. And it's a bargain at two thousand five hundred francs, everything included. You interested?"

"In theory, yeah," Philippe replied. "Can we talk it over?"

"How about a coffee? Let me put some clothes on and I'll be right there."

Five minutes later, Philippe and Robert were crossing Boulevard Jourdan, walking alongside Parc Montsouris on the way to the Porte d'Orléans.

Robert strode along, his shoulders keeping time beneath the old tweed jacket he'd put on. He walked like a cat: nimble and strong.

"You an early riser?" he asked Philippe.

"Not really."

"Like good food and good wine?"

"I'd say so, yeah. Sometimes even a little too much."

"I smoke a lot. Goddamn Gitanes, too."

"So do I. But I stick to Gauloises Blondes."

"I'm rarely home during the day. The apartment would be all yours."

"Great."

"To be honest, you'd have the place to yourself during the day, but I often have friends over at night. To work, or to drink and party. It usually goes on pretty late."

"That's no problem."

They were approaching a café when Robert suddenly stopped in his tracks. Philippe stopped and turned to look at him, intrigued. Robert was staring hard at him.

"You got anything against Jews?"

"Pardon me?"

"Jews, you know, the circumcised guys who walk around wearing skullcaps and are always going on about the Shoah? You got anything against them?"

"I don't think so, no. I'm circumcised, too."

"You're not an antisemitic neo-Nazi, a revisionist, or a white supremacist, are you?"

"No, of course not. Why are you asking me that?"

30

"You're sure you've really got nothing against the Jews?"

"I already said I didn't. Can you just move on?"

"Glad to hear it. I'd have been sad to have to smash your face in."

"Duly noted. But if ever I'm struck down by a bad case of antisemitism, you should know I used to be a boxer. Smashing my face in might be harder than it looks."

Robert burst out laughing and wrapped an arm around Philippe's shoulder.

"I think you and me are gonna get along just fine. The name's Robert Moranowitz. My friends call me Mora. Just don't call me Bob."

"Fair enough. We'll forget about Bob. I'm Philippe Bordeleau. My friends call me Philippe. I get all riled up whenever people call me Phil."

"Got it, Mr. Ex-Boxer. So, how about that coffee then?"

Chapter 7

Lanaudière, October 2002

It's best to sleep on things, they say. Philippe, who hadn't slept at all the night before, didn't know what to make of the saying. His nighttime reflections had left him with nothing but a strong sense of unease, a sharp pang of guilt. Madeleine had been right: the whole thing was ridiculous. Sure, he felt like he owed Mora one last favour and, sure, an eagerness for revenge was gnawing away at him. But he was still a 40-year-old father. A poor excuse for a father, to be precise.

All the same, before leaving home at dawn, he had taken the time to kiss his kids on the forehead, tousle their hair, tell them Dad was going on a trip and would be back in two or three days, promise. A promise he intended to keep. The children had gone straight back to sleep, with the indifference that only the young can have, and Philippe had found himself alone, face to face with his regrets.

The headlights pierced the darkness with their long white strokes. The sky was charcoal grey, covered in cloud from one end of the horizon to the other, although there were now hints of dawn to the east. The temperature was only just above freezing, and the bare fields were coated in a fine film of frost. Traffic on Highway 40 was sparse and in no hurry. The gentle purr of the car's engine combined with the stream of warm air against his face, dulled his senses enough to draw a yawn. To his right, Mora slept, his head resting against the window, his body wrapped in a thick blanket.

Thick drops of water were starting to break against the windshield when he passed the sign for his exit. He turned on the wipers and nudged his copilot with his knee.

"Time to wake up. We're in Berthier. What do I do now?"

Mora gave a start, then began to mumble something. He ran a hand through his hair a couple of times and turned to Philippe.

"Take the exit for Berthierville, turn right, then follow the signs for Saint-Gabriel-de-Brandon."

"Maybe now would be a good time to fill me in on what's going on. Where exactly are we going?"

Philippe lifted his foot, went down through the gears, and took the exit ramp.

"To a cabin by a lake in the middle of nowhere, where there's no one, we hope, apart from the guy we're looking for."

"And who's *we*?"

"Me and Christian, a young guy who's been helping me for a few months. He's already there, keeping an eye on things."

"That's it?"

"Plus you. That makes three, eh?"

"That's a hell of an army. A down-and-out activist, a sick guy who feels the cold, and a youngster who's no idea just how much shit he's stepped into."

Mora waved impatiently.

"Being all cynical doesn't suit you. Leave that to the old farts like me. First off, Christian is well aware of the situation. It's not as if we're gonna ask him to attack a bunker with a bazooka. He's taking care of the research side of things: photo recognition and seeing what our friends get up to on the Internet. Because they have websites and everything, can you believe it?"

"You're joking."

"No joke. Their political positions and philosophy might be straight out of the Precambrian, but they're on the cutting edge of technology when it comes to communications. They've put a global network in place, each layer covering their tracks more and more. Get to the deepest, darkest layer, and that's where you find our good friend Wolf, more active than ever."

"Naturally. So where do I go now?"

"Turn right at the next intersection. After that, you can speed up again. The road's fine until Saint-Norbert."

The rain had stopped, and something approaching sunshine was clearing a path through the thick mass of cloud. Philippe turned off the wipers and motioned for Mora to go on.

"So," Mora added. "We've found out that Wolf has found himself a lair, a cabin in the woods. He's likely hiding guns there, but he's doubtless lying low and coming up with new plans."

"And what are you planning to do exactly?"

"For the moment, wait."

"Wait."

"Last I heard, all there was in the cabin were two bums and a girl off her head on heroine. So we'll wait until Wolf shows up."

"Fuck me. We could be waiting a while."

"Oh no! Didn't I tell you?"

"Fuck off."

For an instant, Philippe saw a flash of the bad streak inside his friend that he hadn't seen for an eternity.

"Don't worry," Mora went on. "It shouldn't take too long. If you've been paying attention to the news, you'll have noticed a little action in the News in Brief column two days ago."

"What kind of action?"

"Two young Blacks beaten up by a gang. And less than 24 hours later, a bad case of arson at a shelter for immigrants that left two dead."

"I did see that go by. There's a link between the two?"

"We don't know right now. But it might be the start of something. And then last Saturday, in an attack that looked for all the world like the work of a biker gang , there was an explosion in a pole-dancing club. Three dead and four wounded."

"And?"

"One of the dead was a left-wing activist who'd been keeping tabs on Wolf. His informer had set up a meeting with him there."

"An unfortunate coincidence?"

"That's not what I'd call it. The activist—his name was Ross Clayton—belonged to a group that follows the far right, neo-Nazis, racists, militia, and other fanatics. One of the things the group specialized in was stopping them meeting up."

"And how do they manage that? They ring the doorbell and politely ask them to leave?"

"More or less, yes. The whole group shows up. They're all well built and armed with baseball bats. They can be quite convincing."

"I see."

"Ross Clayton mainly worked in Alberta and Ontario. He was stubborn and painstaking about his work. When he found out that neo-Nazi cells were forming in Montreal, he moved there. Unfortunately, that was his last case."

"May he rest in peace. But what's the tie to Wolf?"

"The attacks bear his hallmarks, I'm sure of it. That's always how he goes about things. You know that as well as I do. It's the tried and tested tactic of the far right. They spark incident after incident until people feel less and less safe, then start calling for a stronger police presence, for more money to be put into law and order, to toughen up laws and mete out harsher punishments, slowly clamping down on our basic rights and pushing us into the arms of totalitarianism."

Philippe couldn't hold back a derisive smile.

"Don't you think you're being a little paranoid?"

"Think what you want. Wolf's behind the operation that killed Clayton. His informer corroborated information that Christian had gathered by other means. He'll explain it to you when you see him. Clayton managed to find out that Wolf was preparing a hit and that the plans would be made in the cabin we're going to be keeping tabs on. All he was missing was a date. That's why he was meeting his informer. Conveniently enough, they were both killed in the explosion. That's so Wolf. The organization, trapping his adversary, the over-the-top response. It's exactly what he was doing years ago: rocking the boat to get everyone on edge."

"Isn't that a little outdated?"

Mora flinched with impatience.

"Do I really have to spell it out to you? If anything, it works just as well today. Especially after the neoliberal brainwashing we've been subjected to for more than 20 years. Direct action on the ground, plus the growing acceptance of the ultraconservative right in politics—as one-twos go, it packs a punch. People have short memories. They've stopped hearing the alarm bells going off, they find the whole thing 'normal.'"

Philippe pulled a face.

"It's not just that people have short memories, Mora. It's also that no one gives a damn about the far right or the far left. Unemployment rates are down, and people are buying $35,000 SUVs, all leased or on credit. They'll be broke by the time they retire. But they don't care. They keep buying their crappy energy-guzzling SUVs, without the slightest remorse."

"Maybe they don't give a damn, but we have five deaths in two weeks on our hands, all the same! And the problem, as you well know, is that the right and the conservatives are flourishing right now, just as the left has vanished into thin air with nothing to replace it. The old safeguards have gone."

The sign announcing a 50 km/h zone made Philippe slow down. He turned towards Mora's long, eagle-like profile.

"No, the real problem is there's only three of us, up against who knows how many crazies."

"There will be more deaths, unless we do something. We need to stop them or they'll kill again, you know they will."

"I know, I know."

"We have no choice. We have to try."

"Yeah, and we'll all end up rotting in hell."

"I'm already in hell. Turn right. And speed up, would you? I'm freezing. Every muscle in my body is killing me. Put your foot down."

Philippe pushed down hard on the accelerator. The engine growled, but the speedometer barely budged.

Chapter 8

Paris, November 1986

Mora's apartment was in the 20th arrondissement, a stone's throw from the Ménilmontant métro station. It was the type of neighbourhood that Philippe had dreamed of, a hive of life and activity. The apartment was on the third floor of a building that had no elevator. There was only one bedroom, but the living room had been kitted out with a futon and a desk for Philippe.

Mora hadn't been exaggerating: he really did enjoy burning the candle at both ends. He would come home at impossible hours and get up at equally impossible times, when, that is, he didn't just take off for days at a time, without warning or explanation. It didn't take long for Philippe to realize that Mora's apartment was a rallying point for all the regulars at the café on Boulevard Saint-Germain. They frequently met up there, leading to rough and ready meals, followed by long discussions washed down with plenty of wine, more often than not Sidi Brahim from "the Arab on the corner."

Philippe had quickly grown used to the new routine, sleeping in late, then going to afternoon lectures, doing his research, or working in the apartment. After that, depending on his mood, he would make a beeline for the café or eat in the apartment, either alone or with friends. Now and again, he would disappear to walk the streets of Paris late into the night. After a few days of this, he'd recovered a little serenity.

Though he couldn't help but feel a little dissatisfied. As soon as he found himself alone, his thoughts would turn to Madeleine. There was nothing he could do about it; he was obsessed. He could take to the streets and walk until he was exhausted, but she still haunted him. He roamed Paris like a bashful lover. Nothing like that had ever happened to him before. He couldn't work out how such a brief encounter had left such a mark on him. He had to see her again.

One morning as Philippe was quietly having breakfast in his tiny kitchenette, Mora appeared in the doorway holding a sheaf of papers, looking as fresh as a daisy. The funny thing was, it was barely ten o'clock in the morning. He gave Philippe a firm and cheerful good morning, picked up the coffee pot from the stove, and poured himself a huge bowl of coffee. He sat down opposite his new roommate. Philippe raised an eyebrow, surprised at his high spirits.

"You're in good form, Mora. What's up?"

"My friend, we've been living together for three weeks now. We've had a chance to get to know each other, to discuss our opinions and beliefs, and I think—correct me if I'm wrong—that at the end of the day, we view the world in much the same way."

"You could say we get along with each other," Philippe replied carefully, finishing off his croissant.

"Laurent had already told me plenty about you, but I wanted to draw my own conclusions before getting down to business. You follow me?"

"Not really, no. What are you getting at?"

"I have a job for you. Something serious. You have the right profile for it, and I think you'll likely be interested."

"I already have a study grant. I don't want to work on anything other than my thesis."

"It's not about the money, it's about something much more… fundamental. I know you don't have any lectures today, you were no doubt planning to get some work done. But forget about that. I have a better suggestion. First, let's talk a little about *you*."

"About me?"

"I liked you the first time I set eyes on you, but there's no point trusting a first impression. In my line of work, it's best to know who you're really dealing with. So I asked a few resourceful buddies of mine to put together your CV for me."

"What are you on about?"

It was as though Philippe hadn't spoken.

"How about a little coffee for starters?"

Mora picked up the coffee pot to top up their bowls, offered Philippe a cigarette, and plunked one between his own lips. He lit both of them and then, at last, picked up the papers he'd set down on the table.

"Let's start at the beginning. You were born in 1962 in Hochelaga. To a very working-class family. Early on, you showed an aptitude for school, sport, and being a rebel. You discovered your first real passion when you were 15: football. You played all the way up to university level, with the McGill Redmen. You were never a starter, but you were known for your fierce determination. That just about seems to sum it up, since you managed to get ejected twice for fighting, and that's on top of being suspended one other time by your own team for getting into a scrap with a teammate at training. You broke his nose, even though he was a good 50 pounds heavier than you were."

"Come on, the guy was a racist prick! He kept going on about francophones. He called me a 'fuckin' frog' once too often."

"Relax! You don't have to defend yourself. This isn't a courtroom."

"It sure sounds like one. How do you know all that anyway?"

"That doesn't matter. May I go on?"

"Do I have a choice?"

"Not really, no. Let's move on to another aspect of your life. From back in your Cégep days, you were involved in student movements and a handful of organizations whose political leanings were as radical as they were muddled. Then in 1982, you founded the McGill Students' Movement for Québec Independence, a small group that never had more than two members. You went on to join the Montreal Citizens' Group and the think tank For a New Kind of Socialism, two organizations that you quickly left again. Next, you got involved in the student movement against tuition fee hikes, you worked with various organizations fighting poverty and homelessness, you went along with radical feminists as they threw pots of paint at strip joints in the dead of night. On one of those little outings, a bouncer had the bad idea of attacking one of the protestors, so you stepped in and smashed in the face of a man who—let's be clear—was rather thickset. A real killer, aren't you, Philippe?"

"Ah, ah, ah…"

"A life of blood and thunder. Perhaps even a little too much, since your hotheadedness soon drove everyone away. You left groups as soon as you joined them, your friends become more distant, and your last relationship really had seen better days when you decided to go do a PhD in France and start a new life. That's just about all I have. Did I forget anything?"

Philippe sighed and held his bowl of coffee.

"Apart from a couple of bar fights, no. Where did you get all that? Are you working for the RCMP?"

Mora burst out laughing.

"Do you really think the RCMP could piece something like that together? Or CSIS? You're kidding, right? No, I already told you. I have a couple of buddies who are real professionals. They know where to look."

"And just who are your friends?"

"Guys just like you and me. They're not too keen on the direction the world is headed these days."

"Mora, I'm not following you at all."

"Ever heard of the Aryan Nation?"

Philippe frowned and reached for his pack of cigarettes.

"A group of American neo-Nazis, right?"

"Just like the good old Ku Klux Klan, the White Aryan Resistance, the Church of the Creator, the Posse Comitatus, and the most violent of the lot, The Order. Those are the kind of little jokers we're dealing with in the States. But have you heard of the Canadian League of Rights, the Nationalist Party of Canada, or the Aryan Resistance Movement?"

"They don't ring any bells."

"Weeds know no borders, my friend. They go wherever the wind takes them. Well, the same goes for stupidity. In a nutshell, those groups in the United States and Canada are worried that the white race is on its way out. The more violent among them put themselves through paramilitary training, pick fights, and think hanging's too good for Jews, Blacks, gays, immigrants, and communists. They idolize Hitler, cast doubt on the Holocaust, and are convinced that the Jews are pulling the strings of Western governments and the media. The real crackpots among them are gunning for RaHoWa."

"And what's that?"

"Racial Holy War."

Philippe groaned in disgust.

"Europe's also crawling with right-wing extremists and neo-Nazis, minus the religious fanaticism," Mora went on. "They're in Germany, Scandinavia, Belgium, Italy, England, even here in France. None of them are keen on the Jews, obviously, but when it's time to pin all the world's ills on someone, the Arabs will do just fine, or the Pakistanis, the Indians, or the Africans."

"Why are you telling me all this? They're crazy. We both know that. Why do you care what they think?"

"I'm a Jew, in case you forgot. A Polish Jew, to be precise. My grandparents died in Treblinka. So when some moron goes around saying that the ovens are nothing more than some story, and when he'd like to exterminate me while he's at it, I can't help but want to rip his head off."

"I get that."

"And that's just the tip of the iceberg. Because for every one working out in the open, spreading propaganda, handing out leaflets, and trying to get elected, there's a ton of individuals keeping what they're up to to themselves and forming small, independent cells that are hard to pin down. Their goals are more radical, and they're prepared to walk the walk. Beatings, vandalism, arson, kidnappings, murder, not to mention robbing banks, holding up armoured trucks, stealing weapons and explosives... and I could go on. They're getting all excited as they see terrorism on the rise in France, they can see the potential for growth. Which is why we're trying to track them down."

Philippe stubbed out his cigarette.

"It's worrying, I'll give you that. But what's it got to do with me?"

"That's up to you. Are you ready to stand by and watch things steadily get worse, watch society slip back into fascism, or are you going to step in and stop it? It's your call. But one thing's for sure: you have exactly the right profile of someone who can give us a real helping hand. I have a few things that should give you a better idea of the kind of people we're up against."

Mora stood up and walked out of the kitchen. He came back a few seconds later, carrying what appeared to be a heavy cardboard box. He set it down on the floor and moved it towards Philippe with his foot.

"Check this out. I'll come back this afternoon and we can talk it over, okay?"

Mora left without waiting for a reply. Philippe couldn't speak in any case.

The box was full of files and photos. There was a videotape, too. Philippe hesitated for a moment. Then he lit a new cigarette, picked up the first folder, and opened it.

Chapter 9

Lanaudière, October 2002

With the village of Mandeville behind them, they took to a narrow, winding road that bore through the dense forest. Try as he might, Philippe couldn't top 80 kilometres an hour. Farms and homes were scarce, each more run-down than the last. Some 15 kilometres further on, they reached a rough dirt track, its potholes full of muddy water. The car's suspension creaked and gravel crackled against the bodywork, while branches scratched and whipped at the car windows. They drove around a large cabin-lined lake then, five kilometres further on, a smaller lake with fewer homes.

They had driven halfway around the second lake when Mora motioned for Philippe to take a narrow road that ran right between two mountains, stretching out like a dark tunnel beneath the dense trees. The track was full of rocks that pointed skyward like teeth ready to bite, and Philippe needed both hands to keep the car on the road. Despite his delicate approach, now and again a rock would scrape against the car's underbelly with a sinister crunch.

Thirty minutes later, they emerged into a clearing that looked out over a lake, and Philippe stepped on the brake. The road ahead split into two, each branch following a shore.

"Take a left. It's longer, but best not to drive too close to the cabin we'll be keeping an eye on."

Philippe passed by the first track with a sigh, turned the wheel to the left, and floored the gas pedal.

"Try not to rev the engine. Sound carries over the water."

As far as Philippe could tell from the rare glimpses of the lake through the trees, three bays came together to form a shamrock. The few cabins seemed to be empty. The road twisted and turned, and the car skidded easily in each tight bend. They wound their way around the first two bays and, just as they began to drive around the third, Mora motioned for him to slow down.

"Turn right here."

"Huh? Where?"

Philippe could see nothing other than a brief gap in the trees.

"Yeah, here. Go ahead."

Philippe swung the wheel around and the car slipped onto a narrow sandy track. After a bend in the road, a short slope led down to a flat plot of land surrounded by conifers. When they got out of the car, he realized it couldn't be seen from the road. Mora extricated himself with a groan. The land fell away suddenly, running down to a somewhat ramshackle cabin. The door and windows were inky black.

"We go in and we leave at the back so as not to be seen," Mora told him.

He clambered up onto the porch and rapped at the door. Nine times in all, leaving a beat between each. A few seconds later, they heard the door being unbolted and it opened to reveal a young man, his face lit up by a relieved grin.

"There you are at last!"

Christian stepped aside so they could enter.

"Come in, come in."

He was in his mid-twenties. Tall and scrawny, he wore his hair short and sported a beard that seemed less for looks and more the result of a few days of neglect. Pale green eyes darted around behind small oval glasses.

"Christian, Philippe," Mora said, nodding in Philippe's direction. "Philippe, Christian."

They shook hands, but Christian's eyes only briefly met Philippe's. Because he was shy or nervous, Philippe couldn't say. He stepped inside and took a look around. To his left, there was a tiny bathroom; to his right, a kitchenette set off from the main room by a short counter. Next to the bathroom was another room, its door closed, a mezzanine above it. And a little further on, a glass door opened out onto a porch with chairs, a table, and a bookcase overflowing with books and magazines.

"Apart from the bedroom, it's the only place for a little me-time," Mora remarked, following Philippe's gaze. "When you've had enough of me being a sick old man or Christian's cigarette smoke, you can always hide out there for a while."

Every window was hidden behind heavy black drapes, making for a sinister atmosphere. The table in the main room had been pushed to one side. Against the wall opposite the counter, two computers, a couple of boxes with wires poking out of them, and a printer waited on folding tables. One of the screens had been switched off. The other showed a large cabin by a steep slope that fell away into the lake. If it hadn't been for the occasional branch moving in the wind, it could have been mistaken for a photograph.

"That," Mora explained, pointing to the computers, "is our friend Christian's workstation."

He walked over to the window and pushed the drape a little to the side, motioning for Philippe to come have a look.

At the end of a treated wood porch, Philippe saw a thick cedar hedge. It was close to two metres high and partly hid the side of the cabin. On the other side of the hedge, a grassy plot sloped down to the lake. The water formed an almost-perfect oval, barely a ripple on its surface. Around the lake stood trees, more trees, and some more trees. Mora let the drape fall back in place.

"As you can see, the place is deserted. At the far end of the bay, to the left, all there is is an empty cabin. To the right, where the three bays of the lake meet, there's a cabin on the side of the mountain. That's the one we're interested in. To see it, you have to go down to the water's edge. The trees hide it from view from where we are. And that's where Christian comes in."

Mora turned and gestured to Christian to take over.

"Uh, yes, uh," Christian spluttered, pushing his glasses back up onto the bridge of his nose. "Right by the lake, I hid two cameras with powerful telephoto lenses in the fir trees. One of them is infrared. The cameras are hooked up to this computer, which records the pictures."

Christian pointed to the screen that was showing the big cabin.

"This way, we have the place under round-the-clock surveillance. Then all we have to do is print out any photos we like."

He picked up a pile of eight-by-ten photos and handed them to Philippe. They were black and white and grainy.

"That's what we're doing for the time being," Christian added, shrugging by way of apology. "We've only been here a week."

Philippe picked up a first photo. He recognized the cabin from the picture on screen. A series of high windows ran all the way along the front. He could make out two bay windows on the side of the building, next to a narrow door. The rest of the cabin was swallowed up by the trees. Twenty or so metres to the left of the cabin stood a large shed. Down on the water, a dock floated on barrels. A boat was tied up there, the outboard motor up out of the water. Five other photos showed the same scene, centred on the cabin, shed, and the dock. Two figures with their backs to the light could twice be made out behind the curtains. Another photo showed two men getting into the motorboat.

"That was our first test," Christian said. "The two of them hopped into the boat and made their way around the bay very slowly, hugging the shoreline, scanning the shore with binoculars. They passed right in front of us without noticing a thing, then they disappeared out of sight. They were back at the dock around 45 minutes later, no doubt having made their way around the whole lake. They moored the boat and went inside."

"That's all we got?" Philippe asked.

"Along with these ones, yes. That's all."

The next photo showed the two men, skinheads, in work boots, jeans, and leather jackets. They were chopping wood while a woman sat on a log with a bottle of beer. She was dressed the same as the men, her long hair covering almost all of her face. The pixels were clearly visible, but Philippe could make out their faces and expressions. Three other photos showed the same people walking around the cabin, and on the last four photos they had, Philippe could see them inside partying.

"As you can see, the photos are good," Christian added with another shrug. "It's easy to see who they are. The only problem is, they're not breaking any laws. They spend most of the day inside the cabin sleeping and getting drunk. They go around the lake once a day to see what they might find, and occasionally they'll go outside to chop wood."

"That's it?"

"That's it. Aside from the fact that anyone would wonder what deadbeats like them might be doing in such a fancy cabin, there's nothing else to be said. It looks every bit like they're waiting."

"And that's exactly what we're gonna do, too," Mora chipped in.

Philippe sighed in exasperation.

"Are you sure this all adds up to something?" he asked.

"He's on his way. I'm sure of it."

"And what do we do then?"

"I don't know," Mora said, flashing an enigmatic smile. "That depends."

"That depends on what exactly?"

"On how things pan out, and on how many of them there are, among other things."

"Mora, this whole thing stinks."

Christian set about scratching his cheek, as though he'd suddenly come down with a bad rash. Mora laughed when he saw him.

"Relax, Christian. The operational side of things is up to Philippe and me. And chances are, we'll just call the police. Okay. I need a nap. The drugs I'm on have me sleeping all hours. I'm pretty sure Christian made coffee. Pour yourself a cup, Philippe. It'll do you good."

He turned and went into the bedroom. Philippe didn't move for a moment. He stood there, hands on hips, staring at the door Mora had just disappeared behind. An unpleasant feeling came over him. The situation was entirely out of his control. It was as though someone had just pushed him down a bobsleigh track. He cursed. Mora was calling the shots, as usual. And, as usual, Philippe realized, he was going to do what he was told.

Chapter 10

Paris, November 1986

The first file Philippe went over was on France, a detailed list of the terrorist attacks carried out there over the past year. Two bombs at Galeries Lafayette and Printemps in Paris on December 7, 1985. Another on the Champs Élysées on February 3, 1986. On the same date, an attempted attack on the Eiffel Tower, but the police intervened in time. An attack on the Gibert Jeune bookstore, February 4. Then, on February 5, at the Forum des Halles. On March 17, in the Paris-Lyon TGV, as it stood in the station. On March 20, a bomb exploded on the Champs Élysées and another was defused in the métro. A long pause ensued, but the attacks picked up again that September: the post office at the Paris city hall, the cafeteria of a Casino supermarket, Pub Renault, the police headquarters, a Tati store. In less than a year, it all added up to 13 dead and 311 injured.

Counting the dead and wounded like that sent shivers down the spine. No surprise, Philippe thought, that the police and the riot police were everywhere, armed to the teeth and keeping a tight grip on everything, most of all unattended baggage. The rising panic, he read in the report, was exactly what the authors of the attacks had been hoping for: directly attacking individuals in the hope that it might lead to collective hysteria, enough to bring about a shift in France's foreign policy, or even in domestic policy.

According to the information in the file, the CSPPA, the Committee for Solidarity with Arab and Middle Eastern Political Prisoners, had claimed responsibility from Beirut for each of the attacks. The previously unknown group was calling for the release of all Arab and Armenian political prisoners held in France. Investigators, Philippe read, believed it to be a front for Islamic jihad. The attacks could be traced back to sponsors in Iran. At the very bottom of the page, an angry hand had scrawled in red ink: "Ties to the Bundle (see file)."

Philippe set down the pages he'd been holding and reached for the next pile. They listed a second series of attacks, less spectacular this time, but just as worrying. Bookstores specializing in gay, feminist, or Third World titles vandalized, their windows smashed or smeared with paint, their shelves demolished. A ransacked printer's. A firebombed apartment. Death threats, beatings, car bombs. Fractures, contusions, gouged eyes, acid attacks, comas. The only common thread between the victims apparently being the colour of their skin or finding themselves in the wrong place at the wrong time.

Philippe counted, for the first ten months of 1986, 23 such incidents. No one knew who was behind three of them, their descriptions followed by question marks. For the others, there was just one name: Bundle. At the end of the document, a comment had been left in the margin, again in red ink: "Information exchanged and coordination with the CSPPA?" Once again, the reader was pointed in the direction of the Bundle file.

Philippe sighed a sigh of resignation and opened the file.

First, he learned that the "Bundle" (*Bund* in German, *faisceau* in French) derived its French nomenclature from the Latin *fascellus*, itself derived from the classical Latin *fascis*, meaning "packet." In Ancient Rome, he read, a bundle of rods known as the fasces, assembled around an axe blade, was carried by a lictor, sworn to protect the magistrates and to execute their decisions (whipping or decapitation, depending on the crime). The symbol was then picked up by the French Republic after the fall of the monarchy, and again by Mussolini when he formed his "Italian fasces of combat" (*Fasci Italiani di Combattimento*), the precursors of the National Fascist Party. Le Faisceau was also the name of the first French fascist political party in the 1920s.

A chart on the following page set out the branches of the current-day Bundle, complete with names, aliases, and a handful of photos, most of them bad. Cells had been formed in Berlin, Vienna, Rome, Oslo, London, Brussels, and Paris. The Bundle also had ties to neo-Nazi and white supremacist groups in the United States and Canada, including—Philippe almost dropped the notes—in Quebec. According to the document, their strategy was to make contact with and infiltrate any group likely to share their ideology, then to encourage them to radicalize. There were even suspected ties to jihad. What could a neo-Nazi group have in common with radical Islamists? Philippe found the answer in the very next paragraph: they both hated the Jews.

The pages that followed outlined the main ideas peddled by the far right: nationalist, populist leanings; a return to the West's "true values" (justice, order, and family); defending the interests of those who had been left behind (the middle class, small businesses, blue-collar workers) and the "unsullied elements" of the state (the police and army); fanatical anticommunism; and fighting against immigration, insecurity, and unemployment—three elements that were well and truly linked, they claimed.

In this web of hatred, Philippe went on to read, the Bundle sought to start a far-right revolution. The policy it pursued was known as a "strategy of tension," the goal being to sow chaos and destabilize economic, social, and political structures, forcing the state to clamp down hard on security through a series of antidemocratic measures. Overwhelmed by events, the state could then be replaced by the dictatorial régime that the people would be clamouring for.

As with any biker gang, the Bundle's hard core was relatively limited ("50 to 100 members," the document said), although it did have a number of "school groups." A profession of faith in Nazi values was required to reach the top, along with proof of an initiation demonstrating subservience to the group ("see video cassette"). School group recruitment drew on misfits and delinquents, most of them violent, unscrupulous, and in search of a flag. This was the army that had boots on the ground ("see photos"). Operations tended to be carried out between other attacks, most often by radical Islamists, for maximum impact.

A number of pages were devoted to the man who seemed to be the Bundle's uncontested leader: Hans Wolf, also known as Heinrich Weintraub, Harry Wilson, and Hank Walsh. Likely born in 1950. Although Wolf was in none of the photos, the documents gave Philippe a good idea of what he'd been up to for the past ten years.

In the 1970s, Wolf had been a member of neo-Nazi groups in Germany before going on to found the Bundle in Berlin in 1975, establishing ties with extremist groups across Europe, the United States, and Canada, infiltrating the Aryan Resistance Movement in British Columbia, as well as another, unidentified violent group that was close to the Nationalist Party of Canada in Toronto and Montreal. The Montreal cell had been dismantled following a police operation in 1985. Wolf had then come back to Europe and wound up in Paris in early 1986, where he was now very active, thanks to the wave of terror attacks and the rise of Le Pen's National Front.

A series of documents followed, describing in minute detail, complete with photos, various operations that had been sponsored by the Bundle. Philippe quickly worked his way through the photos. Broken windows, burned-out synagogues, desecrated graveyards, blown-up homes and cars. Individuals held down as they were beaten up. Gang rapes. A man, mouth open and eyes bulging, with a revolver pressed against his temple. A Black man, lynched and hanging from a tree. Another, chained to the back of a pickup truck, his body torn to shreds.

Philippe began to feel sick as he reached for the videocassette, his hand trembling. He went into the living room and slid the tape into the VCR. "Bundle initiation - Berlin" the label said.

The movie had been shot in black and white. The filming was jerky and barely audible. It showed a dark room, its dirty cement walls lined with swastikas. Everyone was masked. A man's back. He was tall, presiding over the ceremony in silence. There was lots of pomp and ceremony, punctuated by professions of faith and Nazi salutes. Philippe could make out no more than half of the German words, but enough to understand that the recruit was swearing to kill his enemies and promising to work toward a new Aryan world. He also swore loyalty to the Bundle and its leader. Then a man was shoved into the room. He was stripped to the waist, hands tied behind his back and a bag over his head. His skin was dark, and the folds of flesh around his waist twitched grotesquely out of fear. He was forced to his knees and his hood was removed. He blinked as his head pivoted from side to side. He jabbered incomprehensibly, shaking harder and harder. To great acclaim, the recruit seized a long knife and held it high in the air. He grabbed the man by the hair and yanked his head back. Then he slit his throat. The man cried out, but he quickly went quiet and the head came away from the rest of the body. The body collapsed loudly to the floor, spasming while the executioner, his hand and forearm covered in blood, brandished his trophy for all to see.

Philippe threw up his breakfast into the toilet. He stayed there, hunched over the bowl for several minutes, his mind swirling every bit as much as his stomach.

Back in the kitchen, he carefully put the papers away and returned the cassette to its cardboard case. He lit a cigarette, eager for the taste of bile to pass.

Despite all the information he'd just taken in, he was still having a hard time getting a handle on what was going on. Who exactly were they dealing with? A growing band of psychopaths, ready to do whatever it took to tip our democracies toward far-right authoritarianism? Or was it just a handful of individuals, violent but few in number? Maybe Mora was paranoid enough to mistake a few isolated acts for the start of more widespread violence? Or perhaps he was right: so many years of peace had left us soft in the head, blind to the signs of impending catastrophe.

Was it really so inconceivable? Philippe wondered.

There was no shortage of causes, after all. Alienating jobs, unemployment, unequal distribution of wealth, no future for young people. The falling away of faith, in God or in humankind; a lack of confidence in politicians, government, and public institutions. A fear of immigrants and minorities. Growing irritation at the homeless and drug addicts who were taking over city centres. The fear of terrorism.

Perhaps more people than might be imagined would welcome an oppressive authoritarian state.

Something had to be done, then. And quickly.

But how?

Philippe had no idea.

"So," Mora began. "Not pretty, is it?"

Philippe had propped himself up against the kitchen table, head in hands, his mind in limbo. He hadn't even heard Mora come in. Outside, the sun was already setting. He shuddered.

"No, not pretty at all."

Mora sat down across from him and lit a cigarette. The brown tobacco smoke stung Philippe's eyes.

"What do you think?" Mora asked.

"I don't know. It's like I just dove headfirst into a septic tank."

"Course, it is. It's bloody awful, and the whole thing stinks. It's normal to feel a bit unsettled. Once you've taken it all in, the anger will come. And that's when I reckon you'll be able to help us with a little cleaning up, Philippe."

"Who's *us*?"

"Me and my friends. The Parisians: Laurent, Olivier, Marie. And the others—Thomas, Meredith, Heinrich, and Liset—who are passing through to give us a hand."

"What about you? What are you in Paris for? To go after Wolf?"

"You could say that, I suppose," Mora growled. "Our paths have crossed a few times, and there are a few scores to be settled. The guy has already done enough to humanity. It's time he paid his debts with a spell behind bars. A very long spell."

Philippe couldn't hold back a smile.

"So you come to Paris, you put a small ad in the paper— 'looking for activists to catch notorious neo-Nazi'—you all meet up and you get to work, is that it?"

Mora laughed.

"Not really, no. We've been trying to set up an international network for years. The only way to fight back against the globalization of hate is to globalize surveillance of the people spreading it."

"And what does it do, this network of yours?"

"Most of the time, we try to find out who these people are, where they live and where they work, who's funding them. Once we have enough intel, we pass it on to the police."

"And when that doesn't work? The rest of the time?"

"Our network has given itself permission to not always operate on the right side of the legal line. That's where guys like me come in."

Philippe winced. Mora held up a hand before he could go on.

"The legal path is rarely the most effective. Do you know how many old Nazis are still living in Canada, totally scot-free?"

"No idea. Too many, I'm sure."

"The worst of it is, there's a whole new generation taking over. The Second World War is behind us, and the ideas of the far right suddenly seem less of a threat, less dangerous. But they're coming back strong, Philippe. They're playing the whole thing down, they're even gaining a little credibility and before we know it they'll be everywhere. They're like weeds: they'll be taking over the place, unless we're careful. Sometimes it takes the right weed killer to wipe them out. I like to think that's what our network's there for."

"And what do you expect me to do exactly?"

"I'm here to do more or less one thing: catch Hans Wolf. I don't care about the small fry. You need to strike the head if you want to get rid of an organization. And the head of the Bundle is Wolf. Our friends can help me find out everything I need to know. They're great when it comes to investigating. Less good at the rest."

"The rest?"

"How should I put this? The field work?"

Philippe arched a puzzled eyebrow.

"Getting your hands dirty."

"You need my help beating people up, is that what you're saying? Isn't that a little sick?"

"That's not what I mean. Sometimes we need to talk to people, go into their homes and rummage around in their apartments, find written proof of what they've been up to. Things can go wrong. I never go looking for a fight, but we need to know how to defend ourselves. What I need is someone who sees things the way we do, someone I can count on when the going gets tough. Just let me know if you're that person."

Philippe scratched his beard and pulled a face. Mora reached out a hand and put it on his shoulder.

"Still not sure, eh? You still have reservations, questions? Go on, spit it out! I'll answer you as best I can. I need your help, so I'll play it straight with you."

Philippe hesitated. A vague feeling he couldn't put his finger on was gnawing at him.

"I don't know," he drawled. "There's something about you, something in your voice… I don't know what to think. Whenever you talk about Hans Wolf, I mean. I get your indignation, I get that you're annoyed."

"We're nothing without anger."

"Sure. But whenever you talk about Wolf, I can hear the hatred in your voice. And that worries me. Anger can be healthy when it gets us to act. But hatred's something else. I know all too well—I've been through it myself—how hatred fools around with our better judgment, and how we can come to regret acting on it."

Mora smiled, bringing out the crows' feet at the corners of his eyes. He held up his hands in surrender.

"You got me! When it comes to Wolf, there's no hiding what I really think. You're right: I hate the man from the very depths of my soul. For what he is, what he's done, and what he's getting ready to do now. You really want to know why?"

"Yeah. I like to know what I'm getting into."

"Good policy. Open a bottle of Sidi Brahim. All this talking's making me thirsty."

"The Moranowitz family lived in Warsaw. They were agnostic Jews, descendants from a long and noble line. Cultured, too. They were wise enough at any rate to send their only son Yakob, my father, to study in France when the German storm clouds began to gather on the horizon. But not wise enough to escape themselves: they refused to leave Warsaw and, at the end of 1942, were put on a train for Treblinka. In France, my father became an industrial mechanic and changed his name, once the war started, to Jacob Morane. Then he met a French girl by the name of Paulette Dubois, a Catholic, although just as agnostic as he was. It was love at first sight and they got married. Once the Germans invaded, they moved to unoccupied France and later joined the Resistance.

After the war, my father thought about going back to Poland. But he quickly decided against it: all his family were dead. He didn't much feel like going to live under communism anyway. He wasn't keen on the spirit of revenge that came with the trials following the Liberation, or the suspicions of the cold war. It especially hurt him to see all the experts and bureaucrats who had been Pétain supporters and collaborators during the war go back to their old jobs as though nothing had happened. So my parents emigrated to Canada, a land with a less painful past that seemed full of hope. They arrived in Montreal in 1950, and that's where I was born, in 1952.

My father found himself a job easily enough and quickly rose through the ranks of the industrial equipment company that had taken him on. He invested his savings in real estate, just as Montreal was at the height of the baby boom. Our family soon found itself free of all financial worries. As for me, apart from the fact that I was big-boned and forced to learn Polish, German, and the violin from an early age, I wasn't very different from the other kids. I felt just as Québécois as the rest of them. The story might have ended there, just another family of immigrants who made a new life for themselves in a new land. But, as is often the case, things were more complicated than that.

When they landed in Canada, my parents became Nazi hunters. They started tracking down the people who had fled to Canada, the United States, sometimes South America. They found the men and women who were looking to be forgotten, then they hounded them, telling their new families all about them, telling the newspapers, their employers, until they resigned or were hauled before the courts. Until they ran off again or, better yet, killed themselves. As my parents always said, as long as those swine were free, it was an affront to their victims.

With the rise of neo-Nazi movements in the United States in the 1970s, my parents set up an organization to keep an eye on the groups that were springing up all over North America. Data and surveillance work. Nothing too complicated, at least not until they came across a group calling itself the Bundle. It was the worst of the lot: the most violent, the most fanatical, but the best organized, too. From that moment on, they only dealt with the Bundle, to the point where it became a real obsession.

I never really followed their Nazi-hunting stories. Besides the principles they were acting on and the reasons they were getting involved, my parents barely spoke about it actually. And I wasn't hugely interested, to tell the truth. I'd been born in Quebec and I felt Québécois, first and foremost, not like a Polish Jew who had immigrated and was still getting to grips with history.

I left home as soon as I could, ready to live my own life. The 1970s were a great time to explore. I was ready to get involved in any movement. Student protests, socialism, Marxism-Leninism, then Trotskyism, defending the French language, Quebec independence, the environment... name a cause and, chances are, I fought for it. A pressure group? I was in it. A protest? I was there in the front row, holding up my sign.

What I wanted, at the end of the day, was for the society I'd been born into to evolve and change, quickly and radically, casting off the conservative values that held it up. I found myself new roots. I was proud to live in what I hoped was a forward-looking Quebec.

In 1978, my parents were found in a godforsaken hole in Ohio, their throats slit. They'd been taken out by the Bundle, without a shadow of a doubt by Wolf himself, although the killers were never found. Can you imagine the shock? I was devastated. I'd always thought what my parents were doing was pointless, childish even, at no risk to themselves, a little like they'd belonged to a bridge club. I'd believed in the power of ideas to change the world. Now suddenly I could see that people could kill for ideas, and could die because of them.

I wanted to understand how something like that could have happened, and why. I started looking into it. Into everything my parents had been focused on: Nazis, neo-Nazis, and the people hunting them down. It quickly became an obsession. I met with specialists, surveillance groups, and all kinds of people with any degree of interest in it. I also reached out to the FBI agent who'd investigated my parents' murder in Ohio. He put me in touch with others, who put me in touch with even more people, and so it went from there. That's how I slowly built a network that could give me the information and the means necessary to achieving what had become my one and only goal: bringing down the Bundle, starting with its leader, Hans Wolf. And, no, I was never thinking summary execution. Him spending 25 years behind bars would do me just fine."

A long silence lingered between them before Mora found the strength to go on.

"So there you have it. You can think I'm obsessed, perhaps even a little bit crazy. A poor fool acting only out of revenge. I prefer to think of it as our duty to remember. To remember all those who suffered at the hands of the Nazis and are still suffering in the name of that ideology. And to remember my parents, too, more than anyone."

Mora went quiet, his eyes welling with tears. Philippe was moved. He scratched his head and cleared his throat.

"Okay. I understand a little better now. And I don't think you're crazy. But I'll ask again: why do you need me if you have such a solid network behind you?"

Mora gave his eyes a quick wipe and put on a broad grin.

"I consider you a friend, Philippe. Someone I can tell whatever comes into my head without feeling like I'm being judged. There aren't so many people like you who take a real interest in others. My life is an emotional desert, you have no idea. I spend a lot of time with people, sure, but they're just contacts, folks I have an interest in keeping in touch with, not real friends. And don't even get me started on my love life: no woman in her right mind would want to spend her life with me. I'm on my own, Philippe. I'm desperately alone."

Philippe leaned into the back of his chair and lit an umpteenth cigarette.

"Don't get me wrong," Mora went on. "I think a lot of you, and that's why I want you to work with me. Our friends here in Paris are very good at sorting through garbage cans to find out information. But they won't go into the sewers. They're no match for some of the rats you meet down there. Thing is, sometimes it takes going down into the sewers to find what we're looking for. That's where I come in. If you could come with me and cover my back, I'd feel a whole lot better."

Philippe looked Mora straight in the eye, and Mora held his gaze. His eyes were straightforward, candid. Philippe sighed and rubbed his eyes.

"Fair enough. I think a lot of you, too, but this is a lot to take in all at once."

"Sure it is. You need time to think, to let it all settle. Take as long as you need. But don't forget that things move fast. We need to do something. Quickly."

Mora stood up, and as though only just remembering something, rummaged around in his shirt pocket.

"I almost forgot. Word has it, you're looking for someone. Here you go."

He dropped a folded scrap of paper onto the table and left without a word. Philippe unfolded it with trembling hands. Madeleine's name was written on it, followed by a phone number.

Chapter 11

Lanaudière, October 2002

Philippe had tried to read the newspaper that Mora had brought along, but he put it back on the table after five minutes, unable to find any interest in it. His loud sigh made Christian turn around.

"You need to be made of strong stuff to read the paper," Christian told him.

"Sure. And you shouldn't follow guys like Mora around without having a real good reason to, right?"

Christian nervously pushed his glasses back up onto the bridge of his nose and went back to his screen.

"Absolutely."

"Would you like to tell me exactly what you're doing here?"

Christian shrugged.

"You must have a reason, no? Frustration? Anger? Revenge?"

"Not even. To be honest, I don't know what I'm doing here. Or I no longer know, I should say."

Christian turned around. He stretched out his legs and folded his arms. His eyes met Philippe's.

"You know, for the longest time my life was all about reading the morning newspaper. You learn all about the terrible things that are happening day after day, you read about them, it makes you angry, and you want to do something about it, but you don't do a thing of course, and the whole thing starts over again the next day. Until you take

66

a step back and stop reading the paper. I could never manage to look away, or throw the newspaper out. So I thought I should get involved, make my own modest contribution to a better world. I joined a few groups. Unfortunately, I'm not the best at planning meetings, going to demonstrations, and shouting slogans. I.T.'s my thing. I'm better at downloading protected files or reading emails I'm not supposed to than protesting. It didn't feel right trying to be a protestor."

Christian paused and lit a cigarette.

"And then one day Robert introduced himself. Much to my surprise, he rattled off a list of what I'd studied and other things I'd been doing, the forums and discussion boards I was active on. I don't know what surprised me more: that he knew all about my life or that he was interested in me, just another nameless pawn in the game. Then he told me what he was doing, the people he was following around. That's when it clicked."

"Why that and not something else?"

"Because it was hands-on, real. Completely terrifying, but that made having to get involved even more pressing. And I could be useful. These people are very well organized when it comes to I.T., they're really on the cutting edge. And that's exactly what Robert asked me to do: follow the ins and outs of their networks and decipher their communications. Hate groups have always used whatever media they had at their disposal. It's no surprise they're online. They've set up hundreds of chat groups. They have all sorts of mailing lists and message boards, and they use email too, most of it encrypted."

"May I?" Philippe asked him, pointing to his pack of cigarettes. Christian nodded.

"And then there's the Internet, of course. The first hate site, Stormfront, was set up in 1995! Since then there have been more than anyone can keep track of. They have whole catalogues of crazy brochures and books to order online. You can order any kind of swastika you can think of, SS division lapel badges, Nazi party membership badges, Wehrmacht helmets. Looking for a copy of *Mein Kampf* or *The Protocols of the Elders of Zion*? It couldn't be easier. A couple of clicks of the mouse, a credit card number, and it's in your mailbox two weeks later. Need a Molotov cocktail recipe, a napalm grenade, or a pipe bomb? It'll take less than two minutes to find. *The Anarchist Cookbook*, it's called, and it's free. And that's only scratching the surface. The people Robert is interested in aren't idiots. Their latest strategy is to form a group of small, isolated cells. In North America alone, I've found over a hundred cells that communicate and coordinate their actions online."

"The spark for all of this was when you tracked down the Bundle at last, right?"

Philippe and Christian turned to Mora, who was leaning against the bedroom door. His shoulders sagged and his face was crumpled. He looked exhausted, despite having slept for two hours.

"Any coffee left, guys?" he yawned.

"Sure is," Philippe replied. "It's not the freshest, but there's still some left."

"Sounds good. I'm not the freshest anyway. Go on, Christian, keep going. I'm sure Philippe's interested in what you have to say."

Christian lit another cigarette, which sent Mora into a coughing fit. Philippe motioned impatiently for Christian to continue.

"The Bundle managed to infiltrate political discussion groups. They used the websites to send coded messages that looked harmless enough. The messages seem to have been calls for action. By following the messages and the responses to them, I managed to identify 20 or so cells in the United States and Canada, including one in Montreal."

"Most interesting of all," Mora went on as he sat down beside them, a steaming-hot mug of coffee in hand, "is that the one calling the shots goes by the initials, you'll never guess, HW."

"Hans Wolf."

"Got it in one. Hans Wolf. Keep going, Christian."

"So the Bundle is using discussion forums to send orders that don't seem to be aimed at anyone in particular. We know that hundreds if not thousands of people are regularly using the forums. Some reply to messages, and some of them have nothing at all to do with the Bundle, which makes the whole thing even harder to analyze. But there are a number of people who we know have been charged with criminal activity."

"No surprise there," Philippe sighed.

"No, no surprise," Mora agreed. "But how they're communicating makes working our way back up to the people giving the orders that much harder. When one of the tough guys gets caught by the police, all he can tell them is the message he read on a discussion group. Even when we manage to work our way back through the thread, more often than not we wind up at an email address from a university campus, pirated, of course. Besides, the messages are in code, and don't say much, nothing that could be used in a court of law."

"What we're trying to do," Christian went on, "is follow the messages and try to decode them. To work out, for example, what a message like 'The cat is going to eat canaries in Chinatown' might mean. By matching up messages on the forums with events on the ground sometimes we can work out what happened. 'The cat is going to eat canaries in Chinatown,' for example, was the signal to burn down a community outreach centre for Chinese-Americans in San Francisco. When we have enough details, we pass them on to activists we know who are working in the field."

"More beatings?" Philippe wondered, feeling a headache coming on.

"No," Mora replied. "Don't get all worked up. The activists make do with tracking down the addresses, identifying the individuals, and taking photos. Once we have something that will stand up, we tip off the police."

"And does that happen often?" Philippe asked.

Christian looked despondent.

"Not really, no. So far, we've only had three or four arrests. It takes time, this type of work. A long time. What we're trying to do is catch members of the Bundle in any case. That's the hardest part—they're unbelievably careful."

"To be honest," Mora chipped in, "the results were terrible. Until, that is, Christian stumbled across one hell of a message last month."

"It was a real stroke of luck," Christian admitted, not bothering to disguise a clear sense of pride.

"And what was the message?"

"'The eagle is flying to the nest of frogs to prepare the party.'"

"And what's that supposed to mean?"

"It's our friend Wolf getting a little overconfident. A code name he gave himself more than 20 years ago. The eagle is no stranger to SS imagery, as you know, and I suppose he likes to think of himself as a bird of prey, soaring high over the world below."

"'Vulture' might have been more accurate."

"Without a doubt. But Wolf doesn't seem too concerned with how accurate his metaphors are."

"And what's the party?"

"We've been trying to work that out for the past month. All we've managed to figure out so far, is that the Bundle is planning something, something that's going to kick off in 20 places across North America at the same time. Some kind of bloody event that will leave its mark."

"And the nest of frogs?"

Mora chuckled.

"That one really needs explaining?"

"Not Montreal?"

"Yep. Or at least that's what we think. It's not as stupid as it might seem. No one's gonna come looking for him here. Problem is, Montreal's a big place. We have a few people on the lookout, and we've rounded up a handful of activists who pride themselves on finding needles in haystacks."

"Like Ross Clayton?"

"Exactly. Ross and his guys managed to identify a few of the lowlifes and get one of them to be an informant. That allowed us to confirm what we already thought: Wolf was in Montreal planning something. And also to discover this lovely cabin. But to find out more, we needed Christian's help."

"I intercepted another message last week on a tiny forum that the Bundle had never used before, to my knowledge at least. 'After the fireworks on the 28th, the eagle is returning to its mountain nest. From there, soon, it will swoop down upon its prey.'"

"And not in code?" Philippe demanded impatiently.

It was Mora who spoke up.

"The fireworks, we later found out, were a reference to the explosion in the bar that killed Ross on September 28. The mountain nest can only mean here. At least that's what we're banking on. That's why we're waiting for him to show up."

"That's all you have?" Philippe exploded. "You can't be serious."

"According to Clayton's informant, it should only be a day or two."

"And when he shows up, *if* he shows up, what do we do then?"

"We'll keep a close eye on what's going on. Then we'll see."

"You'll round up your network?"

"What network?"

"Uh, your network. That international network of yours, the people keeping an eye on the crazies, the men and women looking out for the free world and democracy. Who else do you think I mean?"

Mora burst out laughing.

"There's no network, I'm afraid. Or rather, there's no longer a network. The network you are referring to has been gone for a good 15 years."

"What do you mean, there's no longer a network? Clayton and the others, what are they?"

"Oh, they're folks I know, guys I'm in touch with, but no more than that. You're looking at my network. It's the three of us!"

"Are you kidding me?"

Philippe jumped to his feet, absolutely furious. Mora raised a calming hand.

"I'm not kidding anyone. It's just us three. What difference does that make? It's plenty for all we have to do."

"And what exactly is it you're intending to do?"

Mora flashed him a sad little smile, but his eyes lit up like a flare.

"You know exactly what I'm gonna do."

"Mora, you're out of your mind."

"That's what I've been telling you over and over since yesterday."

"What you're planning is nothing more than settling old scores. That's not what you were telling me."

"We already had this same conversation 15 years ago, if I remember right. And back then that didn't seem to be a problem for you. Rooting out the weeds, Philippe. That's all I've ever cared about. Destroying the Bundle and its leader. You've always known that."

"There are specialists when it comes to weeds, people who are paid to go about their work, and who are way better equipped than we are."

"So what do you propose? Should we call the police?"

"Exactly."

"Even if we managed to convince someone to come by and have a look, they wouldn't find a thing."

"Isn't that cabin of theirs meant to be an arms cache?"

"I'm sure it is. But you don't think they've piled them high on the kitchen table, do you? They're probably buried in the woods somewhere. Have you seen the size of the forest around here? When the police leave, Wolf and the others will disappear off into the woods. They'll hide out someplace we don't know, and they'll start over again. Is that what you want?"

"I don't know what I want anymore. I get the impression you're just fighting fire with fire, that you're trying to bring an end to the disorder and unrest through even more disorder and unrest. You're playing their game, Mora."

"What do you mean, 'disorder and unrest'? Isn't everything disorder and unrest? Don't you know that? The whole universe is nothing but disorder, from one end of it to the other. That's just how it is, and there's not a damn thing we can do about it."

"You're out of your mind."

Mora burst into thundering laughter, but it faded quickly. He suddenly looked exhausted, his voice no more than a whisper.

"You're only realizing that now?"

Philippe shook his head and turned away, hands on hips.

"Guys!" Christian said. "Sorry to interrupt, but we have a visitor."

Philippe and Mora turned to face the screen that Christian was pointing to. They saw, as usual, the outside of the cabin. The sky was covered in clouds, and it was dark. Lights had come on inside, and smoke was coming out of the chimney. A shadow passed in front of a window and the side door opened. A pickup truck was crawling across the land that separated the cabin from the shed.

"Zoom in!" Mora shouted, lips pursed.

Christian swung into action and suddenly the truck took up all of the screen. Two men stepped out of it. They scooped up heavy-looking big black bags and walked over to the cabin.

"Follow them, follow them!" Mora cried.

The camera shuddered as it pivoted to the cabin door, where three others were waiting. They all hugged, then went inside. After that, there was nothing but shadows moving behind the drapes, silhouettes of bottles being uncapped and clinked together.

"The little birds are beginning to return to the nest," Mora mumbled with satisfaction.

His face was drawn, but he was thrilled. Weary and apprehensive, Philippe slumped into an armchair to watch the screen.

"We'll just wait, I suppose," he added. "There's not much else to do."

Chapter 12

Paris, November and December 1986

Philippe had been struck by the lightning bolt that goes straight for the nerves. There was a bubbling in the pit of his stomach, and his powers of reasoning had melted away, now in thrall to his senses and feelings. Love is a strange thing, he thought to himself.

Perhaps out of instinct he only tried his luck with women who were sensitive to his charms. But the fact was, his charms won the day more often than not. There was no secret to his success: he went about it passionately, giving it his all. Few women could resist; they were attracted to him like moths around a light bulb. And they tended to get burned, because Philippe didn't know how to control his flame or make it less powerful. He had only one setting: maximum intensity. And so a few weeks later, or even the very next morning, the woman who had found him so charming would often lay down her arms, totally exhausted.

It's too much, you use up all my energy, I need room to breathe. Philippe had heard all that and more. A prelude to putting a little distance between them, or running away entirely. Philippe was intense, he knew that. It was just how he was, the only way he knew. Hence a string of flings that went nowhere. The frustrating, unsettling impression of flitting from one flower to the next, before inevitably finding himself alone again.

Not this time, he told himself. Not this time.

He phoned Madeleine. She was surprised, but seemed happy to hear from him. Philippe managed to talk her into going for a meal in a restaurant he'd just discovered by the Seine.

Packed in tight around the other diners, his head spinning at the clatter of the plates and the knives and forks, conversation flying from all sides, the waiters marching back and forth, he let her talk. He kept himself in check. Not this time, he thought. He stayed safely behind a wall of good manners.

She talked about the boyfriend she'd left behind in Montreal. About their life over there, about her leaving. The uneventful routines of life as a couple, the comfort and security. Then, without even realizing, she slowly let her guard down and opened the door a crack. She vented a little, frustrated at disappointments and built-up resentment. Suddenly it all came pouring out. She talked about how she kept wanting to scream, to cry out in rage at the inertia of her day-to-day life. The boredom was suffocating. That's what had brought her to Paris: the promise of freedom.

Another bottle of wine arrived. Philippe's head was starting to spin; his heart was pounding. He wanted to kiss her, love her, devour her, dissolve himself in her. But he kept a hold on himself. Not this time. Madeleine told him about her new life in Paris, the unending pleasure of new discoveries and newfound freedoms, her eyes sparkling all the while.

Then, suddenly, her face darkened. In no more than a few weeks, she'd have to go back. To Montreal.

A long silence came over them, thick and heavy despite the racket all around them.

He couldn't hold back any longer. The dike sprung a leak and it all came spraying out like a geyser, a volcano erupting. His tongue and his hands couldn't stop moving, his whole body came alive. He talked and talked in one uninterrupted torrent, wave after wave of words. He was swallowed up by the passion that was eating him whole, driving him toward her. He wanted her. All of her, now.

He brought her back to the apartment. The bumps and jolts of the métro, the unending sidewalks, the packed streets, the dark tunnel of a staircase that went up and up. Then everything exploded. He let himself go, he took her and let her take him, he made love to her with all his heart and all his soul. She wanted him again and again. The night was short, but it went on and on. He couldn't get enough of her body, exploring its every fold, venturing into its curves, hollows, hills, and valleys in equal parts Sunday stroll and race to the finish.

The following morning found him spent. And surprised: she wanted more. She wanted all of his passion. She wanted to take it and devour it, draw it in. She wanted *him*.

It was a strange feeling, as though he'd found himself before a vast snow-covered plain. Shades of the absolute, which was new to him. Love. It must be love. Feeling full and satisfied. And nevertheless still wanting more. He loved the feeling. And he loved her, too. A promise, a pledge, bound by blood. He plunged into Madeleine's neck. Forever, he thought.

Philippe was sitting in front of the computer, trying to write his thesis. He really needed to get going on it, but he couldn't concentrate. He was distracted. His brain kept wandering off on tangents.

He thought of Mora. Over the past few days, he'd gone about his business as though nothing had happened, as though the box of files, photos, and the vile videotape hadn't brought them together around a terrible secret. Philippe was excited by the idea of getting involved, but also uncertain. He was unclear what exactly Mora wanted him to do, and unclearer still about what that might involve. He didn't have the courage to bring up the matter himself, so he waited for Mora to make the next move.

His thoughts drifted back to Madeleine. Already a week had gone by since their meal by the Seine. One week, six nights. The six craziest nights of his life. The lack of sleep was wearing on his nerves. And it wasn't over. He was going to see her again that night.

He looked at his watch. Four in the afternoon. He tried to write some more. But what he'd typed only minutes earlier had been reduced to gibberish on the Macintosh screen. His assumptions, assertions, rebuttals, and references were all going nowhere. And none of it seemed to matter. A thought occurred to him, as though he'd just discovered an unbreakable rule: it was all nothing but disorder and chaos. In life as in love.

He moved closer to his thesis draft and scowled. He was saving his file and getting ready to switch off the computer when there was a knock at the door.

He opened it to find Laurent standing there, grinning from ear to ear.

"Hey, buddy! I'm not disturbing you?"

"Not at all. Come in, come in."

Philippe stepped aside and Laurent fell onto the futon with a sigh.

"What's up?" Philippe asked, sitting down across from him.

"First of all, I'd like to apologize."

"Apologize? What for?"

"I made it sound like I didn't know how to get in touch with Madeleine, when I knew all along. But I had no choice. Mora wanted to keep her out of the picture."

"How come?"

Philippe's voice had shot up an octave.

"Let me explain. When Mora realized you were interested in Madeleine, he wanted to… how should I put this? Keep her in reserve?"

"He wanted to use her as bait? Jeez! I was moping around for ages. He had no need to do that."

"I know, but when Mora wants something, he tends to think the end justifies the means. He can get a little hamfisted."

Philippe grunted.

"How do you two know each other, anyway?" he asked.

"He turned up in Paris one day. He introduced himself and said we should shift things up a gear. He can be very persuasive, as you know. He's a leader. He really knows how to get people pulling in the same direction. And then he has the contacts and the resources to go with it."

"You don't seem very into the whole thing?"

"That's fair to say. Since he's been with us, things have gone a little too quickly. Now I'm wondering how we go about our operations. Mora has unbelievable energy. He drags everyone along behind him, but there's no time to think about him making the decisions."

Philippe tried to take on board everything Laurent had just told him.

"He told you his story, I'm sure. What do you make of it?"

Laurent sighed before giving his beard a good scratch.

"Oh, I believe it. The broad strokes, at any rate. But there are still a lot of grey areas. Who are the contacts he always goes on about? Where did he get his money from? And what the hell is this 'network' of his? No one knows, but there are all kinds of rumours. The CIA? Mossad? Jews with plenty of money?"

"The more I hear about it, the less clear everything is."

Laurent shrugged.

"Sorry I can't tell you any more. We're all feeling our way through the fog, and he's the captain of the ship, accountable to no one. He might be a genius, or just a madman, but so far it's working. There have been arrests, some people have disappeared back into the woodwork, and we've found others to keep a close eye on. We're getting results, in other words. It's your call, if you can live with that."

Philippe nodded, deep in thought.

It was right at that moment that the front door opened.

Mora loomed in the doorway. Thomas hovered behind him.

"So," Mora began, walking over to Philippe. "Ready for a little adventure?"

"What kind of adventure exactly?"

"Well, something's brewing, but we don't know what. We'd know more if we paid a few of our friends in the 15th arrondissement a visit."

"When? Right now?"

"We're just leaving. Otherwise it'll be too late."

"But I'm supposed to be going out with Madeleine tonight. I don't know if—"

"It'll only take an hour or two. Are you in or not?"

Philippe struggled with the question, to which he had no answer. He quickly found himself back where he'd started: he didn't know where it all would lead. And there was only one way to find out."

"OK," he said, his voice hollow. "I'll get my coat."

Laurent parked the Peugeot 504 on the street and left the engine running. Thomas fidgeted beside him. Both sitting in the back, Philippe and Mora looked calm and relaxed, even though Philippe was bubbling with nervous excitement. Mora leaned over and tapped Laurent and Thomas on the shoulder.

"It'll be fine, don't worry. If we're not back in 20 minutes, get out of here and call the police. Okay?"

The two men agreed, then Mora turned to Philippe.

"You don't say a word. Anyone speaks to you, you grunt. You follow me and you let me get on with things. If things go south, you follow your gut. Okay?"

Philippe rolled his shoulders back, trying to relax, before pushing the air out noisily from between his lips.

"Okay by me."

"Good. Let's go."

They got out of the car and strode down the sidewalk. Fifty or so metres later, Mora stopped at the entrance to a building and pushed on the buzzer beside the door. He pushed open the heavy wooden door. They both stepped into a dark stairwell.

"Don't touch the light," Mora hissed. "The darkness could come in handy. It's on the third floor. I hope you're in shape," he laughed.

"Don't you worry about me," Philippe said.

When they got to the third floor, Mora walked up to the door on the left and put his ear to it. They could hear the deep bass of rock music. He nodded with satisfaction.

"Good. They're home. You ready?"

"What are we doing again?"

Mora flashed him an enigmatic smile and rapped on the door. Three times in quick succession, then two longer knocks.

Footsteps could be heard behind the door, followed by the sound of two bolts being drawn, then the door opened to reveal a round, brutish head with closely shaven hair and piglike eyes.

"What is it?" the man asked suspiciously, trying to peer through the darkness of the hall.

"Just a check," Mora replied. "May I?"

He put his hand against the door and gave it a shove as he walked into the room. The man stepped aside to let him pass.

"Yeah, of course."

Philippe followed him inside to the main room. The man who had opened the door gave him a halfhearted hello. Philippe just growled.

The room was full to bursting. Files were strewn over a table, and metal filing cabinets, their paint flaking, had been pushed against a wall. Swastikas hung from flags and banners around the room. Two other men were there. One was carefully working with something in a duffel bag. The other was standing, leaning back against the window, arms crossed. He reached out a hand to turn off the stereo and took a step toward Mora. Instinctively Philippe positioned himself between Mora and the man who had opened the door.

"What's going on?" spat the man who'd stepped toward Mora.

He was tall and thickset, but smaller than Mora. Despite his efforts to show that he was in charge, he had to look up to glare at Mora, which seemed to irritate him.

"We've just come to make sure everything's going well," Mora said nonchalantly.

His hands were in the pockets of his raincoat, and he looked around the room like a prospective tenant.

"What are you talking about?" the other man asked. "There was to be no contact with anyone until tomorrow morning."

Philippe could sense that things were going to take a turn for the worse very quickly. His heart was pounding in his chest, and cold sweat ran down his neck. The man opposite Mora looked to be worked up, and he didn't seem like the type to hang around asking questions. The second man zipped the duffel bag closed and eyed Mora up and down, while the third man hovered by the door. Out of the corner of his eye, Philippe saw him take a step toward them. Philippe took his hands out of his pockets and folded his arms, then took a nonchalant step to his left so that he was standing in his way.

"Of course not," Mora replied in a strangely quiet voice. "But there's been a slight change of plan."

"Forget it!" the man opposite Mora roared. "I'm not changing a thing. I take my orders from Hans and no one else! I've got a job to do and I'm gonna do it, period. I don't know who you are, but you can fuck right off."

"Hans isn't going to be happy."

"That's my problem."

"He's going to be furious, but not for the reason you think."

The other barely had time to frown before Mora had delivered a furious right jab that landed square on his chin.

"Uuh!"

The shout came from the man standing behind Philippe. Without thinking, Philippe turned around and charged at him, head down. His shoulder made solid contact with the man's stomach and took both of them into the metal filing cabinet, which squealed under the impact. Philippe sent out a blind right hook and his fist ricocheted back off the man's temple. The man groaned then, fighting to get his breath back, he replied in kind. Philippe parried the blow with his left forearm, then grabbed him by the collar, flinging him against the filing cabinet. Hurling himself at him, he delivered another right, which landed on his nose. He heard the bone crack, followed by a cry of pain. Philippe kept going with an uppercut that hit the man below the jaw. His opponent's head rolled back under the blow, and Philippe could feel the man grow heavier in his left hand. He let go of him and the man dropped to the floor, unconscious. He felt a pull on his shoulder and whirled around, ready to strike back.

"Hey! Calm down, it's only me."

Mora had both hands raised in surrender. Behind him, the two other men were on the floor, unconscious. Philippe dropped his hands and rubbed nervously at his face. The skin on his knuckles was raw, but he couldn't feel a thing. He was warm, the blood was thumping at his temples, and he was wheezing more than breathing. He leaned back against a filing cabinet and let himself slide back on his heels. Opposite him, an enormous flag with a swastika on it hung from the wall, a black and white photo just beside it showing a dense crowd, right arms extended in salute. Philippe was hyperventilating.

"Relax," Mora told him. "I'll take care of the rest. There must be some rope or something in this dump."

Mora walked around the room, pulling on a pair of surgical gloves. He produced another pair from his pocket and flung them at Philippe's feet.

"Put these on. You can't be too careful."

Philippe caught the gloves. Mora crowed with satisfaction and bent down to pick up a heavy roll of electrical cable.

"Just what I was looking for."

He walked over to the first man and bound his hand and feet, moving on to the next man when he was done.

Philippe put on the gloves, picked himself up, and went over to the duffel bag. Inside he found a small clock, wiring, metal parts, and greasy cardboard cylinders. Sticks of dynamite.

"Jesus!" he shrieked, scrambling back to his feet. "A bomb! They were going to plant a bomb."

Mora had his back to him as he tied his knots. He didn't bother to turn around.

"What did you think? They were bringing bread and jam to their grandmother? We knew there was a bomb. But we didn't know who it was for or when it was going to go off. That's why we needed to move right away."

"Fuck!" Philippe muttered. "They're crazy."

He paced around, trying to calm down, but it only made him angrier.

"Right! That's that," Mora said, as he finished tying up the third man. "Let's see if we find anything interesting while we're here."

He went over to the table that was covered with pieces of paper and began reading through them. Philippe kept pacing around, unable to collect his thoughts.

"Bingo!" Mora cried a few minutes later.

He held up a sheet of paper to show Philippe.

"I found what we were looking for," he beamed. "Let's go."

He dragged Philippe by the back of his coat over to the door. Philippe followed Mora like a robot and left without looking back at the three men lying on the floor.

One minute later, they were closing the doors of the Peugeot behind them.

"Well?" Laurent asked, peering back at them in the rearview mirror.

"Three men," Mora replied, "and just as we thought, a bomb."

"Three of them? Wow, you guys are strong."

"I'd watch out for Philippe, if I were you. He has a hell of a right hand on him!"

He gave Philippe a friendly tap on the thigh. Philippe shuffled closer to the door. He didn't feel very well, all of a sudden. His head was spinning and he was incredibly thirsty, as though he'd just swallowed a barrowload of dust.

"So what now?" Thomas asked.

"You get out, find a phone booth, and call the cops."

Thomas got out and ran off from the car.

"Laurent, you're gonna bring Philippe and me here to the closest métro station. Then you can take care of this."

He passed him the piece of paper he'd found in the apartment.

"Nice! A list of Bundle hideouts. That's worth its weight in gold."

"It is, but hurry up and get it to our contact with the police, because tomorrow morning it's not gonna be worth a cent. Let's move."

Laurent gunned the engine by way of reply.

Mora turned to Philippe and handed him a bottle of water he'd just picked up from by his feet.

"Knock some of this back, it'll do you good. It always feels like that the first time. You get used to it, you'll see."

Isn't that the worst of it, Philippe thought to himself.

Chapter 13

Lanaudière, October 2002

Philippe was already on his third coffee. Despite the hopes that had been raised by the pickup showing up the day before on the other side of the lake, the rainy Sunday morning had passed by without incident. The only thing worthy of note was that there were now five individuals walking around inside the cabin they had under observation. Early that morning, one of them had set down two crates of beer on the back porch. Two others had later gone outside to chop wood. They'd gone back inside, too, and that had been that.

Time was ticking on.

Christian had taken photos of everyone, eight-by-ten close-ups from the front and side. They all looked the same. The same jeans, sweatshirts, and leather jackets. And the same pale faces of night owls who shunned daylight and came into their own by the light of the moon. They gave them all nicknames, to keep things straight. The short, pudgy one: Fatso. The tallest of the bunch, with the arms of a gorilla and thin bow legs: Cowboy. The one who looked like he'd been blown up with helium and wore everything three sizes too small: Mr. Muscle. The latest guy to show up, with a long hooked nose that his fingers were never out of: Snot. The girl they called Junkie.

"Cowboy, Mr. Muscle and Junkie are getting into the boat," Christian reported gloomily, his eyes trained on the screen.

"Snot is back on the dock, scratching his balls," Mora chipped in, peering over Christian's shoulder.

"Fatso must be back in the kitchen eating his chicken wings," Philippe added from the end of the veranda, where he'd retreated to.

The waiting was getting to their nerves. Mora drank one cup of tea after the other, muttering to himself. He was in a foul temper, a real bear with a sore head. He kept hiding out in the kitchen, playing solitaire on the counter. Which, needless to say, did nothing for his patience.

Christian stared blankly at his computer screens, smoking cigarette after cigarette. He passed the time consulting his files and arranging his photos. When he'd had enough of playing around with his photos, he opened his chess game and let the computer wipe the floor with him.

Philippe, meanwhile, had scoured the cabin's only bookcase and come up with only one book worthy of interest. It was the title of Hemingway's classic *For Whom the Bell Tolls* that had caught his attention, but the writing left him cold. He kept setting the book down and going over to bum a cigarette off Christian, which he then smoked without pleasure, stubbing out the butt and returning to his stodgy novel.

The day just wouldn't end. Nothing moved. Suddenly Mora could take no more.

"Jesus Christ! What's he waiting for? What the hell's he doing?"

He took his frustration out on a folding wooden chair that found itself in his way, demolishing it piece by piece. He finished it off with one final kick that lacked conviction, then threw himself onto another chair that groaned beneath his weight. He was dazed and out of breath. Sweat was pearling on his face.

"My God," he sighed. "I'm an old man."

Philippe set down his book and went into the kitchen to make another pot of tea. He came back with two mugs and handed one to Mora.

"Thanks," Mora replied, wrapping his hands around the mug.

Philippe picked up a chair and sat down opposite Mora, folding his arms around it.

"Mora?"

"Interrogation time?"

"Call it what you want. But there's something I want to know."

"I'm listening."

"Are you sure Wolf is really up to something?"

Mora shrugged.

"I think he is, but I'm not 100% sure. What would he be doing here, if he's not?"

"Maybe he's putting his feet up? Getting away from it all."

Mora gave a mirthless laugh.

"Guys like him don't go on vacation. Getting up to no good is a full-time job. And what idiot would come here on vacation in October?"

"Good question. I was just asking myself exactly the same thing. Maybe he's come here to hide out, no more than that."

"Could be. But what difference does it make?"

Philippe ran the back of his hand across his stubble, producing an unpleasant scratching sound.

"Well, if he's come here to hide, maybe it's because they're looking for him?"

"Who? The police? Of course they're looking for him! What difference does that make? He's spent most of his life on the run."

"Okay. Say it doesn't change a thing. But if he is just looking to hide, maybe he doesn't really have a plan. I'm not so sure when I see the state of the people hanging around that cabin. What could he be up to with a bunch of weirdos like that? Are they going to be out stealing beer? Cracking open P.O. boxes?"

"I don't know, Philippe. I told you, we don't know what he's planning."

"I think you're taking me on a ride. Are you sure the guy's still a threat? Is there even still a Bundle or are we up against two men and a dog who think they're killing machines?"

Mora sighed and stretched his legs.

"Okay. The Bundle has seen better days, I'll give you that. There's no comparison with the network of 15 years ago. But that doesn't mean Wolf can't still do damage. They killed Ross Clayton, remember, and there's been at least a dozen attacks over the past two years that can be pinned on the Bundle. But I already told you, it doesn't change a thing. It's Wolf we're interested in. No more Wolf, no more Bundle."

Just as Philippe was opening his mouth, Mora cut him off by jumping to his feet.

"I'm starving! Ham sandwiches, everyone?"

Philippe cursed, but Mora had already turned away.

Chapter 14

Paris, December 1986

"You need to be careful he doesn't twist your whole arm off," Madeleine said.

It was four o'clock in the afternoon. The sun was already weaker, and the thinly spread light of the cold December day was taking on an apocalyptic tint. The apartment that Madeleine shared with a girlfriend in a suburb to the south of Paris was vast by French standards. The many windows that ran all the way along the three rooms looked out over a large wood. But it was dark in the bedroom, and Philippe and Madeleine instinctively clung to each other beneath the tangled sheets. All that could be seen from the window was a muddle of bare branches that formed a sinister scene.

"What do you mean?" Philippe mumbled, struggling to fend off the waves of sleep that were washing over him.

"Mora's nothing more than a manipulator. I know he's a smooth talker. He can be convincing. But he's still a manipulator. You should keep your distance, before you back yourself into a corner."

"Why do you say that?"

"Because it's obvious! He's not crazy, but he's not far off."

Stung by Madeleine's remark, Philippe sat up against the wall.

"Now you're going too far."

It was Madeleine's turn to sit up.

"I don't think so, no. He sometimes has a strange glint in his eye, haven't you noticed? It's frightening to see. He looks like a killer."

Philippe thought for a moment, then set his hand down on Madeleine's thigh.

"You're right. He can be intense. And when he gets like that, it's as though he's capable of anything... I'm fascinated by him. He has the natural authority of a born leader, the ability to influence people, get them to rally around a common cause. I've always wanted to change things, and I don't think it's the energy I'm lacking, but I don't have what it takes to get people to rally around me. With him, for the first time in my life, it's like I'm taking part in something that's really going to get results. Where's the harm in that?"

"Where's the harm in that?"

Madeleine sighed and stepped out of the sheets. Philippe's eyes followed her naked body. She took her pack of cigarettes from the table at the far end of the bedroom, lit one, then turned to face Philippe, half sitting on the table, arms folded beneath her breasts.

"I suppose he got out a big box of files, full of all kinds of information on neo-Nazi groups and Hans What's-his-name, complete with photos and horrible videos?"

"How did you know that?"

"Because he did the same with me. I talked it over with him a couple of times. You're right: he's a smooth talker. He makes everything so clear and exciting. It's a little unsettling how easily he gets you all caught up in it, too, and talking to him makes you feel like you're more intelligent. I was angry as well when I saw what was happening to the world around me. Maybe that's why he thought I was fit for service."

"Did he try to get you into bed?"

Philippe felt stupid for asking. But he couldn't imagine Mora spending a whole evening with a woman without trying to sleep with her.

"Not even. Sure, he pulled out all the stops, but it was only a potential recruit he was trying to win over. He turned up at my place with a box of files one day and left them with me to read. I couldn't sleep for two days. I told him I wasn't interested. It was the day after I met you at the café. That's why I never went back. I was pissed at not seeing you again, but I didn't want to get caught up in his schemes."

"How come?"

"Because I don't think we should be fighting fire with fire. We have the police and the courts to deal with people like that."

"Are you kidding me? Do you really think the far right are worried about the police? You do know that the National Front gets tons of recruits from the police and the army, right?"

"Don't start going on like a broken record. What Laurent, Thomas, and the others are doing is fine. It's perfectly legitimate civic responsibility. But when Robert is in charge, they play by different rules. That's what Thomas told me. Ever since Robert set foot in Paris, they're no longer in control. And they're worried."

"Mora's only acting like that because there's no time to waste. Lives are at stake. We need to get our hands dirty, we don't have a choice."

Madeleine stubbed out her cigarette. She crossed her arms again and stared hard at Philippe.

"And when will enough be enough?"

"When they're all in prison."

"It's never over, can't you see that? There will always be people saying terrible things, spreading vile political opinions, and killing people because they think their skin is too dark. You want to take them all on? How do you think that's going to end? With some great peace treaty once the battlefield's been cleared? Or a never-ending war, an armed struggle between left- and right-wing militias, each taking the law into their own hands? I can't believe what I'm hearing, Philippe. It feels like I'm listening to an old newsreel from the 1930s!"

"I'm not the one turning to the 1930s for inspiration, I'd like to point out."

"Oh, don't be stupid. It's not gonna end well. That's all I can say for sure. It's going to wind up in a bloodbath, one way or another."

"That's exactly why I'm getting involved—to avoid a bloodbath."

Madeleine groaned and ran a hand through her hair.

"What did you do last night?"

He looked away.

"Huh? Oh, nothing special."

"Considering how worked up you were when you came to see me, I have a hard time believing that."

"Nothing special, I said. Mora and I went to get some information, that's all."

"Philippe, if there's one thing I can't stand, it's lying."

"You're right. I'm a terrible liar."

"So?"

"I went to visit an apartment with Mora."

"To visit an apartment?"

Philippe nervously scratched at his beard before going on.

"Okay. You really want to know? We paid three men a visit. It gave us information that should prevent a good bit of damage being done. When we left, we called the police to come pick up the three guys."

"You're kidding, right? You knocked on their door, they opened, and they asked you to come inside and take whatever you liked?"

"Not like that, no. We didn't ask their permission and we didn't give them time to protest."

"My God, have I fallen in love with a psychopath?"

"There was a bomb! They had a bomb and they were getting ready to plant it."

Madeleine walked over to the bed and flopped onto the mattress.

"Be careful, Philippe," she gasped. "What you're up to can't be worth it."

Philippe felt stupid. He could see, when he put it like that, how their visit must seem like they'd been settling a score, wrapped up in nothing but meaningless moralizing. It was fighting fire with fire, she was absolutely right.

But there had been a bomb. If they hadn't gone to that apartment, the morning newspaper would have been full of reports on the injured, the maimed, the dead. Was that reason enough? He was less and less sure. Perhaps he should tell Mora he wouldn't be tagging along with him any longer. Or perhaps learning to lie with a straight face would be easier.

Philippe slid back underneath the sheets. He moved his hand across and gently rubbed it across Madeleine's back.

"When are you leaving for Montreal?" he asked her.

"Two weeks on Friday."

"It won't be long. Are you coming back?"

"I don't know. I'm not sure anymore."

"Tell me we'll see each other again."

She looked him in the eye.

"That depends on you. As far as I'm concerned, nothing's keeping me in Montreal any longer. I just need to go back and sort out my things. Maybe after that I'll feel like coming back to meet up with you. But what state will I find you in?"

"I'll be just the same as I am now."

She pulled back the sheet that had been covering Philippe and straddled him. She ran both her hands along his chest. Philippe had a low-angle shot of her chest and began to sense that he was in trouble. Madeleine worked her way down his abdomen to between his legs, then took him in her hand.

"I hope so. Because I'm very fond of you, you know. And I'd like to find you in one piece when I get back."

She leaned in until their lips touched and Philippe felt himself getting bigger in Madeleine's soft, warm hand.

In the days that followed, Madeleine and Philippe had the same discussion several more times, making the same arguments from a different angle or a little more eloquently. But the result was always the same: deadlock. Day after day, as the tension rose, their relationship began to come apart. Philippe realized he was becoming more and more vehement, and Madeleine was hardening her position, growing colder and more distant. He kept trying to convince her to put off going back, or at least to come back soon. She remained vague, promising that she'd call and write, but had to sort a few things out first. She needed to think.

Madeleine was hurtling away at eight hundred kilometres per hour over the Atlantic, and nothing had been resolved.

Each of them could now mull things over at their leisure, Philippe told himself. Which is what he did all that afternoon, staring out the window from his futon as the grey clouds filed across the Paris sky like a flock of mangy sheep. Worn out and demoralized, he cursed his stupidity. Not for the first time, his hot temper and unwillingness to compromise had ruined everything. The woman he had thought was the love of his life had just walked away, and he hadn't managed to hold her back or get her to promise she'd return.

That very same evening, Mora called on Philippe again. Philippe was unenthusiastic, but he tagged along without hesitation. They went to a slovenly apartment, then to a small warehouse. Mora had what they needed to force the uncooperative locks. Philippe had no idea where and how he'd learned how to do that, and didn't much feel like asking. All he felt was a furious urge to bury his fist into the face of the first person to stand in their way. If there happened to be a dozen guys standing in their way, he'd only feel all the better for it. His face no doubt betrayed his baleful intentions— Mora had already cast him a worried glance or two—but Philippe only grunted in reply.

The breaking and entering part might have been easy, but the results were a letdown. The place was deserted. There was no one to rough up, nothing but books and documents.

Mora brought a few of them back to the apartment and set them on the table where Philippe worked.

"Make yourself useful," he snarled. "Try to see if we can get anything out of this crap. Clues, names, anything at all."

"And what are you gonna do?"

A tense smile came over Mora's lips.

"Blow off some steam. Visit the seedier side of town. Get drunk, get laid."

Philippe wasn't sure whether to take him at his word, but Mora disappeared for four days.

All too aware he'd missed his deadlines and hadn't kept a single promise he'd made to his supervisor, Philippe used the time to get back to work and finish the first draft of his thesis. Once he'd handed it in, he found himself alone again, at his lowest ebb.

He found some wine in the fridge and sat down at his desk to write to Madeleine, a short letter he wrote and rewrote three times. Then a fourth. He wasn't any happier with the fourth version, but since he didn't think he could do any better he promised himself he'd mail it the following day.

He had nothing to do. He didn't feel like eating or watching TV. Let alone picking up one the economics articles that were eyeing him from their shelves. Not even like reading a novel.

He noticed the pile of papers that Mora had left on the desk. Curious, he nudged them closer. They were short articles. Some were from magazines he'd never heard of, while others were short texts, typewritten then photocopied. The titles spoke volumes.

"The Revolution is Now!"

"Equality: Man's Most Dangerous Myth"

"A Great Man: Adolf Hitler in Perspective"

"The Meaning of the Swastika"

"White Nationalism and White Power"

There was also a novel: *The Turner Diaries*.

The first article began with a quote from *Seven Pillars of Wisdom* by T.E. Lawrence, better known as Lawrence of Arabia and considered to be the father of modern guerilla warfare. "An example to be followed," according to the article's author, who then went on to set out the key role played by the media in bringing about sweeping social change, providing examples of the control exercised by the Catholic Church through the mass distribution of the Bible and the control exerted by the Jews via a stranglehold on mass media.

In the second article, a man claiming to be a doctor tied himself in all sorts of knots in an effort to convince readers that racial differences of genetic origin were much greater than cultural differences. Philippe pushed the article away, unfinished. He skipped the next article, not feeling up to reading a Hitler apologist, skimmed through the article on the swastika, and passed on the others, an insufferable hodgepodge of the greatness of the Aryan race and the strategies to be employed to ensure that it regained its rightful place: at the very top of the human pyramid, needless to say.

As for the novel, penned by a certain Andrew Macdonald, it wasn't exactly the work of the century. Philippe read enough of it to see that it was about a world revolution led by a "white" army that was working toward the extermination of Blacks, Jews, homosexuals, and other minorities.

Philippe tossed the novel away, resisting the temptation to indulge in a little book burning. Instead he went into the kitchen, uncorked a bottle of Sidi Brahim, and poured himself a glass. Sprawled on the futon, he tried to gather his thoughts.

By leaving the documents with him, had Mora been trying to teach him a lesson or had he just been looking to strengthen his resolve against the men and women who proclaimed such monstrous things? He looked for an answer in the bottom of his glass, but found only excuses for more distractions that eventually led to troubled sleep.

December 24, 8 p.m.

Philippe was gearing up to again lose himself in second-rate alcohol when Mora swept into the apartment carrying a bag of groceries. He was angry, bubbling over with barely suppressed rage, ready to go off at the slightest provocation.

Mora asked Philippe if he was hungry, then disappeared off into the kitchen. He made merguez, pasta with pesto, and broccoli. A meal worthy of the Sidi Brahim, Philippe thought.

Mora ate without saying a word, still furious. Philippe pushed his plate away and decided to strike up a conversation.

"So?"

"So?" Mora growled.

"I mean, what's up?"

"Nothing."

Philippe let the silence settle back down over them. After a minute that went on forever, Mora noisily put down his knife and fork and lit a cigarette.

"He's toying with me."

"Wolf?"

"Who else?"

"How come?"

Mora filled their glasses.

"I've been acting alone these past few days because I was afraid he might be laying a trap for us. And to be frank, given your current state of mind, if I'd had you with me, I'd have felt like I was walking around with a grenade with the pin pulled out."

Mora raised his eyebrows.

"Am I wrong?"

Philippe winced.

"Listen, Madeleine's gone and I'm not even sure if she'll ever come back. I'm in a bit of a funk."

"Need to talk?"

"Forget about it."

"Whatever you want. You know I'm here, right?"

"Thanks, that's nice of you. Right now, more than anything I need to think about something else. So, what's been happening the past few days?"

Mora looked hard at him, as though weighing up his state of mind. A few seconds went by before he nodded.

"Okay. I picked three addresses at random from the list we found the other day, and I went by to have a look. The police had already been, of course, but I thought that things might have picked up again three weeks later."

"And?"

"Nothing. Other than they were clearly expecting me. No alarm, doors just about locked. Nothing of interest, apart from papers like the ones I left you. And each time: this."

Mora stood up and produced a rolled-up t-shirt from the grocery bag he'd left on top of the fridge. He threw it on the table. Philippe picked it up and unfolded it. A black eagle was printed on a red background, a swastika in its claws.

"Nothing special, eh?" Philippe said.

"Have a look at the other side."

Philippe turned the t-shirt over. It read, "Adolf Hitler European Tour, 1939-1945," followed by the names of countries and the date they'd fallen to the Nazis. The last line read, "1987…?"

"Slightly more original, I'll give you that."

"That's why I said he's toying with me," Mora continued. "He's taking me for a ride while he goes about his normal business. I can practically hear him laughing at me."

Mora dropped a handful of newspaper cuttings onto the table.

"You saw this already, I suppose?"

The articles were about an attack that had been carried out the previous day. A bomb had gone off in a local bakery, leaving one dead and seven injured."

"Of course I did, just like everyone else. What does that have to do with Wolf? The articles say it was a group of Arab extremists."

"That's what I would've thought too, but for one small detail."

"What's that?"

"The dead man was in the Bundle."

"What?"

"What's even more disturbing is that he and I often had little chats."

"You had a mole in the Bundle?"

"It's all about being in the know!"

"It must be a little dangerous, though?"

"He was the one who wanted to play both sides. The day before yesterday, I went to check out a place that wasn't on our list. An address that my informer had given me. No one was expecting me, there was no t-shirt. All I found was a few guns and some ammo. I spray-painted "Death to the Nazis" on a wall before I left. Childish, I'll give you that, but I wanted Wolf to know I'd been there."

"And the next day, by a stroke of bad luck, your mole goes to buy a baguette and it explodes underneath his arm?"

"Exactly. The graffiti wasn't the brightest thing I've ever done. Wolf doesn't have much of a sense of humour, by the look of things. And I've been left high and dry."

Although the anger was still smouldering in Mora's eyes, Philippe could also see something he'd never seen there before: doubt.

"What are you going to do?" Philippe asked, offering him a cigarette.

Mora took it distractedly, a cloud of blue smoke enveloping the two men like a protective cocoon.

"I still have an ace in the hole," Mora drawled. "I hope so, at least. Either way, it doesn't matter if it's an ace or not. It's the only card I have left."

He looked up, waiting to see how Philippe reacted.

"And what's your ace?"

"I met with my informant, before Wolf dealt with him. We had words. He gave me an address. I think it's one of Wolf's personal hideouts, somewhere he probably has drugs, weapons, cash. We could really hurt him."

"And why would this address be more valuable than the others?"

"Because my guy wasn't supposed to know it. He only found out after following Wolf around Paris for days."

"And what if Wolf knows that, too?"

"If he does, then I'm in trouble. But it's either that or I pack my bags and go back to Montreal. It's a risk I'm prepared to take. What about you? Are you in?"

Philippe and Mora were crouched in an alleyway that ran perpendicular to the street. Mora pointed at the building opposite them, a business whose pink façade clashed with the drab grey of its surroundings. A glass door stood next to a large window. Both glass surfaces were covered with brown wrapping paper, with only a glimmer of light escaping from between the creases in the paper. A half faded sign revealed the store had once been a hair salon. The street was deathly silent, the quiet barely interrupted by the muffled whish of the cars speeding by on the Périphérique in the distance.

"What do you think?" Mora asked.

"How do you want me to think anything? It looks deserted, that's it. Normal enough at four o'clock in the morning, no?"

"Pass me the bag."

Philippe slid the backpack off his shoulders and held it out to Mora. It was heavy and compact. The sound of bottles clinking together echoed into the night.

"What's inside?" Philippe asked.

"A bit of calvados to see out the night," Mora told him. "Check there's no one around, would you?"

Philippe stepped forward and stuck out his neck. Hemmed in by tall grey buildings, the street was dark and silent.

"All good. Not a soul in sight."

Mora turned his back to him and plunged both hands into the bag.

"Got a light?"

Is this really the time for a smoke? Philippe wondered. But he dug out his pack of cigarettes and tossed his lighter to Mora. Mora caught it and went over to Philippe.

"Still good?"

Nothing but shadow and silence, the regular cones of the street lights and the cracked reflections against the windshields. Philippe gave the all-clear.

Mora had Philippe's lighter in one hand and, in the other, two bottles with a rag sticking out of the top. The strong smell of gasoline suddenly filled Philippe's nostrils, and he looked at the bottles in disbelief.

"I'm going. Watch my back."

Mora sauntered across the street. He stopped outside the door to the building with the pink façade. The click of the lighter echoed around in the street. Two tiny yellow flames filled out in no time, lighting up the night. Mora lifted his knee and kicked hard against the door handle. There was a sickening crack, then the door swung open. An alarm sounded, a pathetic tingle. Mora's arm traced the arc of a circle. Once, twice. Glass shattered, then a terrible whoosh followed by a red flash. Mora turned his back on the show and, hands in pockets, calmly walked back across the street.

An explosion sounded; glass shattered. All around them, shutters opened and lights went on in windows, creamy rectangles against a reddening monochrome. The flames and smoke climbed skyward, burning paper billowing through the air before gliding back down.

"You coming?" Mora hissed at Philippe as he walked past.

Philippe was paralyzed by the spectacle of the flames and the windows lighting up in turn, casting their light over the buildings that surrounded them. Mora tugged at his sleeve.

"You're sure there was no one in there?" Philippe stammered, unable to take his eyes off the blaze.

"What the hell do we care, man? What the hell do we care? Here's your lighter back."

Philippe caught it. It was still warm. Mora bent down and, without breaking pace, scooped up the backpack and pulled out a hip flask.

"A little calvados to warm you up?"

Philippe grabbed the flask and knocked it back. His mind was blank.

Two blocks further on, they heard the firefighters' sirens.

Mora and Philippe looked back. Behind them, the flames were high in the sky, spitting out suspicious-looking black smoke. Another explosion went off.

"Happy Christmas, dear Hans. I hope you like your gift."

Chapter 15

Lanaudière, October 2002

They'd eaten, shared a bottle of wine, then washed the dishes and taken one last look at Christian's screen: no change.

They went back to waiting.

After an hour or two, Philippe went over to sit beside Mora, unable to contain his impatience.

"We didn't finish that conversation earlier."

"Didn't we?"

"One last question…"

Mora rubbed at his face.

"Shoot. That's all there is to do around here anyway: talk."

"What are you planning to do?"

"Wait. What else?"

"Cut the bullshit. I lost my sense of humour somewhere on the way here."

Mora looked up and gave a half smile.

"You know exactly what I plan on doing."

"I'd like to hear you say it, all the same."

"Kill him, of course."

Christian, sitting close by, began to wheeze.

"And how do you intend to go about that? You must have a plan, no?"

"I have a plan. But I'm not sure it holds up."

"Try me."

"Well, considering the state I'm in, there is, by the look of things, only one way to go. Once Wolf gets here, we walk out to the road and follow it over to the cabin. Just before dawn, around four or five in the morning, is right when people tend to be sleeping the heaviest."

"What if there's someone keeping watch?"

"No one's keeping watch. Christian checked with his infrared lenses."

"And what if there's someone that night?"

"We take them out. You can still do that, right?"

"Okay. So let's say I can still do that. Maybe they have a security system: lasers, tripwires, motion detectors, that kind of thing."

"Doesn't matter. By the time they react, it'll be too late. Then we'll be needing this."

Mora stood up and shuffled off into the bedroom. He emerged a minute later with a heavy-looking hockey bag. He set it down on the table, then unzipped it theatrically.

Philippe moved the bag toward him and took a look inside. It contained enough assault rifles and ammunition to launch a full-scale attack.

"Have you lost your frigging mind? What do you think we're gonna be doing? Invading Okinawa? Why not a rocket launcher while we're at it?"

"The thought did cross my mind. But they're hard to get hold of."

"The only time I ever fired a weapon was my dad's 22 Long Rifle. And that was in the woods with no one around."

"Well, we're in the woods now. And unless you consider those sickos over there to be bona fide human beings, there's no one within three miles of us. You wanna know where we go from there or not?"

"Go on."

Mora reached into the bag. He pulled out an automatic rifle, which he tossed to Philippe. Philippe caught it in midair. The rifle was lighter than he'd have thought, and must have weighed only two or three kilos. Philippe held it up to his face. To the left, above the magazine he read: COLT M4 CAL 5.56 mm. The metal below that was heavily scored. No doubt where the serial number had been.

"What's this. Rambo's gun?"

"The very thing," Mora replied. "The M4 Commando is a descendant of the M16, standard issue in the U.S. Army since Vietnam. It's shorter, so it's easier to handle. But you need to be careful: this thing spits out seven hundred rounds a minute. It takes three seconds to empty your magazine. Thirty bullets. It goes in like this."

A metallic click rang out as Mora snapped it into place.

"You load, take the safety off, then you spray."

Disbelief came over Philippe's face.

"That's your shitty plan? We spray them while stocks last?"

Mora's grin broadened.

"You know me better than that. Here's what I propose: Christian gets into position to cover the side door to the cabin, while you and me take the front. We send a few rounds through the windows to give ourselves some room, then…"

Mora disappeared back into the bedroom and re-emerged with a chunky backpack. The clinking of bottles brought back old memories for Philippe.

"Then it's good old Molotov to the rescue! I'll throw two inside through the bay windows. I'm not up to much, but I should be able to throw a couple of bottles in through a window or two. Plus, everything's wood inside the cabin. The place'll go up like a Saint-Jean bonfire. We stick around to take in the show, and anyone who tries to come out, we turn into Swiss cheese. Operation over. We all go back home. I go back to my meds, you to your kids, and Christian to his computers."

Philippe glanced over at Christian, who'd just picked up one of the rifles and was holding it, arms outstretched, as though making an offering to the gods. He was deathly pale.

"By the way," Mora went on. "If it comes to it, there's a shed outside, and an old boat turned over on cement blocks just in front. Inside the boat, wedged against one of the seats, you'll find an assault rifle identical to this one, along with all the magazines you'll need."

Mora paused before going on.

"What do you think?"

"You've completely lost it."

"We knew that already. You have a better suggestion?"

"Not really, no."

"Okay. So that's how we'll do it. Then it's so long, Wolf, you old scumbag. The world will be rid of you at last."

Philippe set down the M4 on the table and walked around, running the back of his hand against the beginnings of his beard. He cleared his throat and turned to face Mora.

"Okay, Mora, okay. Just one thing. You and me go way back. One of the unpleasant things that unite us are the dead who aren't easily forgotten. And there's Wolf, of course. I agree with you. One way or another, it has to end."

Mora waited for the rest, unperturbed.

"But this has nothing to do with Christian. Let's not get him involved, okay?"

Still the same silence.

"He's been very useful. He's done what you expected of him. Now he's no use to us any longer. I'll go buy some groceries the day after tomorrow. I'll take Christian with me and drop him off in Saint-Gabriel. He can get the bus back to Montreal from there."

Philippe's plan was even more precise than that. He'd wait for Wolf to arrive, alone with Mora. When the vulture reared its ugly head, he'd call the police and take off. Knock Mora out if that's what it took, pack him into the trunk and bring him back to town. Too many people had died already. It had to stop.

"Sound like a plan?"

Mora nodded. His head barely moved in something approaching agreement. As though he suspected what Philippe was up to, and couldn't care less. For a split second, Philippe thought he could glimpse his son Lucas's face in Mora's: the stubborn look that came over him when he was being told off, that way he had of hunkering down and waiting for the storm to pass. A face that said: Talk all you like, I'm going to do what I want.

Chapter 16

Paris, December 1986

Philippe sauntered out of Saint-Michel station and walked east along Boulevard Saint-Germain. Once Madeleine had left, he'd returned to his old habits and would head to the café around five o'clock for a beer or two and to clear his head. But the outing was nothing like the fun-filled after-work drinks of the early days. Most of the group's members were getting ready to leave Paris for Christmas or catching up on work. Fortunately, Philippe knew that Laurent and Thomas would be there, two of the regulars.

A sense of unease had been added to the sluggishness that hadn't left him since Madeleine had gone. The malaise, sparked by Mora's firework display, was proving difficult to shrug off. He hadn't dared read the newspapers, listen to the radio, or watch TV. It would have been unbearable to hear that someone had lost their life to the fire that they had started. And he hadn't seen Mora since.

Philippe glanced at his watch. He was a good half hour later than usual. He didn't speed up, though. All around him, the crowds were tightly packed and jumpy. He had to clear a path for himself along the sidewalk. It was another day when it was hard to tell when the sun had come up and gone down. He suddenly realized something: only the sparkle of the snow and the pure, clear sky made the endless Quebec winters bearable. Everything in Paris was grey and opaque. Two months of uninterrupted gloom, and winter was far from over.

I really need a drink, he thought to himself.

Strangely enough, rather than thinning out, the crowd was becoming even more dense. A rumour was growing around him. He caught sight of a column of black smoke rising into the sky. The wail of police sirens and fire engines came at him from all sides. Worried now, he sped up, but he was forced to slow down again seconds later. Barriers had been placed across the street, blocking traffic and leaving cars, horns blaring, in an indescribable state of chaos.

Philippe stood on his tiptoes, trying to see what was happening on the other side of the hundreds of people who were massed ahead of him. A broken window, tables and chairs knocked over onto the road, firefighters and ambulance technicians running around outside his usual café. Panic took hold of him, and he waded into the crowd, paying no heed to the protests of those around him. Progress was slow as he moved strangers out of his way, clearing a path until he reached the barrier and the gendarmes behind it. He looked around for familiar faces, for bodies. All he saw was people lying on stretchers, covered in sheets. He searched for a sign, a clue in the confusion of uniforms amid the shouts and the screams.

Someone tapped him on the shoulder. Thomas. Philippe sighed with relief.

"What's going on?" Philippe asked. "Are you going to tell me?"

They'd walked for a good 15 minutes, steering a course from one side street to the next until they landed in an out-of-the-way bistro. Thomas hadn't unclenched his teeth the whole time.

"A bomb. A bomb just went off in our café. Laurent's dead."

"What? It can't be."

"It can," Thomas replied in a funereal voice. "If I'd been two minutes earlier, I'd be a goner too."

"You're sure about Laurent?"

Thomas poked his glasses back up onto the bridge of his nose.

"Completely sure. I'll spare you the details, but I was able to check."

A moment went by before Philippe was able to open his mouth.

"Did you try to contact Mora?"

"Yeah. A dozen phone calls later, I found him over at Olivier and Marie's."

"What did he say?"

"Find you, keep our heads down, make sure we're not followed, then come wait for him in this bistro."

"Nothing else?"

"Less than an hour ago, the windows of Olivier and Marie's apartment were shot at. That's why Mora was at their place."

"Are they hurt?"

"Nothing serious, just a few scratches. But there's more. Meredith's car was blown up when she was less than 50 metres away. Two men jumped Heinrich and his girlfriend and beat them up. The building where Maurice lives was firebombed. And our café was blown up. At least three dead and ten injured, plus Laurent. All at the same time, perfectly synchronized. The results speak for themselves, eh?"

Thomas's laugh was terrible, like two metal plates grating against each other. Philippe felt sick.

"And Mora?"

"He's fine. He was out all night. Wouldn't tell me where, or what he was up to. You don't happen to know anything, do you?"

The uneasy feeling that had been working away at the pit of Philippe's stomach for two days picked up again.

"We set fire to an abandoned store the day before yesterday. Near métro Javel. Mora wanted to get a reaction from Wolf. I don't know what was in there, but it went up like a box of fireworks."

Thomas scratched his nose, thinking.

"Robert kept saying we needed to flush Wolf out, get him to act on instinct and make a mistake."

"Well, he reacted. Jesus! Laurent… I can't believe it."

Another grating laugh crossed Thomas's lips.

"Mora thinks the café bomb was meant for you, not Laurent and me."

"Me? Why me?"

"What? You're the one that's been getting up to all kinds of things with him, not us! You're his sidekick. You live with the guy. If he'd killed you, Wolf would really have hurt Mora."

"Damn, I hadn't thought of that."

"We're so screwed. Wolf won't think twice. He'll just pick us off, one after the other."

"What are you going to do?"

"I'm going back home to Berlin. I don't want to know how this ends. You should do the same."

"Did Mora say what he's planning to do?"

"Not a word. The only thing he cares about is catching Wolf. And to hell with the consequences. I knew from the second he set foot in Paris that things were going to go bad.

I knew it, but I let myself get twisted around his little finger, just like everyone else. I was under his spell, too. What an idiot!"

Thomas looked up and frowned.

"Here he comes now."

Philippe watched Mora's trim figure approach.

"Robert," Thomas began curtly. "I'm leaving for Berlin tonight."

"Good. That's the best thing to do right now. I've told everyone to go and lay low."

Thomas waited impatiently for Mora to go on, his jaw clenched, a vein bulging in his neck.

"That's all you can say?" he eventually barked after a minute.

"What else should I say? That I'm sorry? That won't change a thing."

"You're such a fucking pain, Mora! Laurent's been killed, our friends have been massacred, innocent people are dead or wounded—"

"We're at war, Thomas. Didn't anyone tell you?"

"It's not exactly what we signed up for."

"That's what war is: we know when it starts, but not when it ends, or how bad it's gonna get. Those are the rules of the game."

"But it's not a game!"

"We got a reaction out of him. That's what we wanted. He reacted and he showed himself."

"No! That's what *you* wanted. It was *your* idea, and you didn't ask anyone's opinion. It's *your* war, not ours!"

Mora leaned down over the table and grabbed Thomas by the arm.

"I'm sorry," he told him, his voice surprisingly gentle. "You're right, I messed up. It was real stupid of me to think Wolf couldn't get to us so quickly. Yes, I know…"

He waved away Thomas's objection with a swipe of the hand.

"There were victims. We'll make him pay. Believe me. But no matter what we did, there would have been victims. You know that."

Thomas agreed meekly, his chin buried into his collar.

"Until now, he's been smart enough to stay behind other people and leave no trace of his own. And it worked: the police looked to other groups, not his. But today he made a big mistake that's gonna let us get our hands on him."

Thomas sighed and opened his arms, hands facing upwards.

"I get it. You apologize, but you're not sorry. The cause comes first, right? I've had enough. I'm out."

Thomas stood up wearily and walked around the table. He strode across the café and was soon out of sight.

"What about you? Are you interested in what comes next, or are you gonna let me down too?"

Philippe was confused. His stomach wasn't happy.

"Shoot."

"First off: safety matters. You don't go back to the apartment again. It's too obvious a target."

Mora put his hand in the inside pocket of his raincoat and produced a business card, which he set down in front of Philippe.

"I rented you a room at a hotel not far from here, under the name Philippe Bélanger. The address is on the card."

"Under my mother's maiden name? Great. What about my books? My stuff?"

Mora gave Philippe a roguish smile.

"Don't worry. I'll have it all moved to your hotel room by people who know how to be discreet. Don't say I don't look after you, eh?"

"Really great."

Mora rummaged around in his raincoat again.

"Pay with this," he told him, sliding a debit card across the table. "The code is on the business card for the hotel. There's enough there for a few weeks. Maybe more, if you don't go crazy. Be careful where you go. Keep your eyes open, don't take the same route. Watch out for strange-looking cars and pedestrians. You should be safe enough. Paris is a big city. It's easy to get lost in."

"Okay."

Philippe pocketed the cards and finished his coffee.

"What about the rest?"

Mora stared at him long and hard before replying.

"You really want to know what happens next?"

"I do, yeah."

"You're sure? You can go, too, you know. I won't hold it against you."

"I'm real sure. I want to get my hands on him, too. Even more than before. It's going to take me a while to get over Laurent being murdered. Someone has to pay."

"You're not frightened?"

"Of course I am."

"Well, at least that proves you're not out of your mind."

"So?"

"Since I set fire to the hair salon, I've been keeping an eye on the place. Wolf must have been furious, so I hoped he'd gather his troops and get ready to hit back. Thanks to my informant, I know a few of Wolf's lieutenants and where they tend to hang out. I staked out the bars they go to, I watched the people coming and going. It was a long, hard wait, but it paid off. Last night I recognized one of his cronies and followed him to a nice-looking building in the 14th. The parade got underway at ten o'clock. They all filed in, one after the other. Brawny guys covered in tattoos, not the type to be doing PhDs in philosophy at the Sorbonne. I counted eight of them and took photos of them all. Then, around midnight, I saw him go in. I saw him, Philippe, I finally saw him!"

Mora's eyes shone as though overtaken by a sudden fever.

"Wolf?"

"Yes, Wolf, that son of a bitch. I'd been waiting for that moment for years. You have no idea how excited I was. There he was, right in front of me, practically within arm's reach. It took everything I had not to get out of my car and knock his head off. He walked up after the others, calm as you like. And I was able to take all the photos I needed. Have a look at this."

Mora handed Philippe a photo. A man was scowling at the camera, hands in coat pockets. The photo was dark, but it was easy to make out Wolf's features. Shaven head and oblong face, a long straight nose, and a bull neck that emerged from the collar of his shirt like the trunk of an old oak tree. It was the look on his face that drew attention. Pale eyes lit up by an animal glow.

"What a charmer!"

"Isn't he just? I waited outside. It was a long wait. They started coming out early this afternoon. In twos, around 15 minutes apart. Each pair with a duffel bag. I managed to take photos of all of them, of their cars, licence plates, the works. They all returned to the fold around five o'clock, then once they were all back, I left to develop my photos. I knew whatever they'd been up to was over. Four targets. I had no idea then if the attacks had been carried out using explosives, fire bombs, or machine guns, but I knew something big had just happened. I didn't know what was going on until Olivier called my photographer friend to tell me his apartment had been attacked with a machine gun. I should have warned everyone last night. I wasn't thinking."

For a fraction of a second, Philippe wondered if Mora hadn't used his friends as bait. The thought terrified him: could Mora be so Machiavellian? Could his thirst for revenge have scrambled his brain to that point?

Mora grabbed Philippe by the arm.

"I know what you're thinking. You're wondering if I didn't let them get on with it just so I'd have proof at last, aren't you? Come on! I'd never have hung my friends out to dry like that. The truth is much more simple, believe me: I screwed up. I'm an idiot. In the heat of the action, when I hadn't stopped for 24 hours, I got carried away and I didn't think. I forgot all about being careful. I'm not proud of it."

Philippe looked at him, not knowing what to make of it all. Mora seemed truly sorry.

"So what do you do now?"

"Wolf's little show is over. He must be feeling nice and confident by now. He'll want to kick on. He won't be able to resist putting the final nail in our coffin. No doubt he has something impressive up his sleeve for us. I'm counting on him feeling smug. He thinks he's in control, that he's routed us. It's up to us to turn that to our advantage. I'll go back to staking them out tonight. With a little luck, he'll turn up with his band of degenerates to plan what happens next. That's what I'm counting on. If you want to tag along, you're welcome."

Philippe closed his fists around the table.

"I'll be there. I wouldn't miss it for the world."

Mora had insisted that Philippe drive the Renault 4. It was a real boneshaker, with no power to speak of, and a gear stick that emerged from the dashboard. In Paris, it fit right in.

Mora had him pull up in a quiet street in the 14th arrondissement. Philippe turned off the engine and they both settled into their seats. It was eight o'clock at night. There was nothing to do but wait. Smoke a cigarette. Munch on a ham baguette. Sip coffee from the thermos Mora had brought along. Have another cigarette. Then wait some more.

An hour later, Mora told Philippe to drive off. They drove around the block, then parked on the other side of the same road, a hundred metres further along. They waited. It was cold and damp. Their noses ran; they couldn't feel their toes. They yawned their heads off, drank coffee until they felt sick, and each lit an umpteenth cigarette. They went for another drive and parked a little further along. More waiting. More yawning.

Midnight. The thermos had been empty for hours. Philippe gave himself a shake and was about to start the engine when Mora grabbed his arm.

"Here we go!"

A man was walking down the opposite sidewalk, a hundred metres away. Philippe and Mora buried themselves into their seats. The man was walking quickly, head down. He was short and mean-looking. He took a quick glance around, pushed on a door, and disappeared inside. Five minutes later, another man who looked just like him walked up.

Eight of them had gone through the door when Mora elbowed Philippe in the ribs.

"Here he is! Here he is!" he yelped.

A tall man was slowly making his way down the sidewalk. He was wearing a long raincoat and an old béret. Despite the distance between them, Philippe immediately recognized the man from the photo that Mora had shown him. The same hulking body, the same broad shoulders and thick neck, the same curved, vulture-like nose. He strode across the street. When he reached the doorway that all the others had disappeared into, he waited outside for a few seconds. His head turned slowly from side to side, scanning for any suspicious sound or movement. Philippe and Mora, despite being over one hundred metres away, held their breaths. At last, Wolf disappeared inside, too.

"I'm gonna knock that son of a bitch off his perch," Mora spat.

He opened the door and stepped out of the car. In the rearview mirror, Philippe watched him race off with the ease of a 400-metre champion. He disappeared around the corner, slipping back in beside Philippe less than two minutes later.

"Right, let's go."

Philippe drove off, moving the car into second gear.

"Take it easy," Mora growled. "No point making too much noise."

By the time they reached the next intersection, a police van was racing towards their Renault 4, siren blaring. A second followed, then others from the far end of the street, all sirens and lights.

Philippe watched the police take up position on the sidewalk. He turned down the next street, leaving the show to play out behind them.

"They were waiting for my signal," Mora gloated.

"You'd tipped them off?"

"Of course. What did you think? You can't wing an operation like that. I know a commissioner who's a bit less of an idiot than the rest of them. He doesn't like it when things are too glaringly obvious. He likes to keep an open mind. Everything we have on the Bundle, including the photos I took yesterday, it's all on his desk right now. He'll enjoy nothing more than bringing them down. Wolf's finished. He won't be hurting anyone else now. My God, I can't believe it. It's over at last."

Philippe gunned the engine into third gear.

"How about a beer to celebrate?" he asked Mora.

Chapter 17

Lanaudière, October 2002

The night had been terrible. All three had slept badly, and their mood was feeling the effects. They'd had breakfast one after the other, no one talking. The mood was heavy and tense, and the wait that just went on and on worked away on their morale like a corrosive on metal. Philippe leafed through his Hemingway novel without conviction, Mora stared at the living-room ceiling as though a great truth was about to come crashing down on his head, and Christian, nerves now frazzled, had gone outside to smoke on the back porch.

Christian came back inside five minutes later. He'd regained a little colour.

"Ah!" he said, trying his best to sound jovial. "It's freezing, but a little fresh air does a body good!"

Philippe and Mora only grunted in reply.

"Tea, anyone?"

No answer.

"I'll make us all some tea!"

Christian set to work noisily in the kitchen, spooked by the silence around him.

Once all three found themselves sitting in front of a piping-hot mug of tea, the atmosphere seemed a tad warmer than before. Mora even allowed himself a little smile.

"What are you smiling at?" Philippe asked him.

"Ah, nothing. I was just watching you and thinking you haven't changed much in 15 years."

Philippe burst out laughing.

"Really? We all change, you know. Our bodies fill out, we lose our hair…"

"I don't mean physically. After 15 years of silence…"

Philippe frowned, and Mora was quick to hold up a hand of apology.

"I know, I know. That was entirely my own fault, but let me go on. It's good to see you, I mean. A lot of memories have come flooding back."

He paused. Philippe just looked at him.

"What strikes me most is finding you so… in one piece. Just the same as you were when we met. So wonderfully naive. I always liked that about you. Now don't take that the wrong way, it's a compliment. You're an idealist! An idealist who, despite the setbacks, remains a committed optimist. You've no idea how much meeting you 15 years ago helped me, and how even today you almost make me want to believe in a better future. I envy you, you know. I'd really love to have just a little of your faith in humanity. Because I don't believe in a damn thing anymore."

Philippe rubbed his jaw, skeptical.

"It's a funny sort of compliment. But you're right: I always like to give people the benefit of the doubt. I've been let down more than once, though."

He hesitated before going on.

"I have memories that are coming back to haunt me too, you know. Good and bad. And sometimes I can't help but think that, just like before, you can call me your friend all you like, but when push comes to shove you're using me. You're using my 'naivety,' to be more precise. To do your bidding, to help you get what you want."

"That's harsh."

"But there's some truth to it, isn't there?"

Mora swallowed a mouthful of tea before replying.

"I did sometimes cut a few corners to speed things up a little. I wasn't being manipulating, just impatient. I can't stand by and wait for things to happen. I need to start them."

"Do you really think of me as your friend?"

"Of course I do! More than that, even: you're the one true friend I've had in 20 years."

"Okay. And you'd agree that real friends should be frank with each other?"

"Sure."

"So?"

"What are you getting at?"

"You could be a little more transparent, don't you think?"

Mora burst into genuine, honest laughter.

"Okay, okay. What is it you want to know exactly?"

"You've always said you're out to avenge your parents' murder, that you hold Wolf responsible. But I don't believe you. You're obsessed. You're so angry, I can't explain it. Because you're never told me about your parents, practically nothing. As though you didn't feel a thing for them. As though you hated Wolf for something else. I don't know what. But I'd like to understand why."

Mora looked hard at Philippe, not blinking. Christian, although he was over at his computer, was taking in every word of the conversation.

Mora broke the spell with another laugh.

"You want to know the truth?"

"It would be about time, no?"

"You won't like it, my friend. And once I'm done, chances are you won't like me much either."

"Go out on that limb, all the same. That's what friends are for: the risk of being frank."

"The risk of being frank! Only you would ever say something like that! And that's why I'm so fond of you."

"Better to live with a painful truth than a soothing lie, no?"

Another guffaw.

"I could smack you one on the lips, Philippe. That's exactly what I meant when I called you naive. The truth, the whole truth, and nothing but the truth! You rise above the hypocrisy. So, fair enough, I'll take the risk of being frank, as you put it. Christian, can you make us some more tea?"

Mora settled into his chair, waiting for Christian to return.

Chapter 18

Europe, Winter 1987

Sitting cross-legged in his tiny hotel room, Philippe watched Mora pace back and forth: five steps in one direction, about-face, five steps in the other. He was furious, muttering incomprehensibly to himself. Philippe had never seen him so angry.

He would have loved to feel such cleansing, liberating rage himself. But instead he felt flat, emotionless, and disillusioned. As though he'd been disemboweled and was nothing more than a slack carcass.

"Can you imagine?" Mora fumed. "The police arrest everyone, seize enough weapons and explosives to blow up half the city—it's the operation of the year—and no sign of Wolf! No one's seen him, no one knows him. As if he never existed. Tell me I wasn't dreaming, Philippe. We saw him cross the street and go through the same door as all the others, didn't we?"

"We did."

"He must have seen us, then. Or sensed something was up. He went inside and left by another door, no one any the wiser. Dammit!"

He lashed out at the chest of drawers.

Philippe didn't have anything to add.

"I'm gonna kill him, you hear me? I'll devote the rest of my life to it, if that's what it takes, but I'll find him and I'll kill him! I'll cut him up into little pieces and feed him to the rats!"

This time Mora punched the frame of the door, which creaked in complaint. He dropped onto the bed.

"We have to start all over again," he added, his voice quivering. "We're all out of clues. Left empty-handed, like two idiots. Wolf's out there somewhere, we just don't know where. I should've gone with my gut instead of trying to be the model citizen."

"And what did your gut tell you to do?"

"Put a bullet in his head as soon as he crossed my path."

"Then you'd be in prison right now. A lot of good that would have done us."

"It would have. I'd have no problem rotting in jail if I knew he was dead."

Mora stood up and began to pace around the room again. But he sat back down after two minutes, exhausted by his own fury.

"What do we do now?"

Mora looked helpless.

"I dunno," he shrugged. "Really, I don't. Wolf must be raging right now, all the same. His whole Paris team is behind bars. I suppose he'll react, one way or another. Unless he runs off and—"

He stopped himself, his forehead scored with wrinkles.

"But that's it. Of course! He'll leave Paris! Wolf's a pack leader, he won't act alone, out in the open. He's lost his cronies, so he'll go off looking for new ones. If not in France, then somewhere else. I'm such an idiot! I'll get on the phone to my contacts in Amsterdam, Brussels, Berlin. We'll see."

He stood up and charged out of the room. Philippe ran his hands through his hair a couple of times, a vain attempt to try to get his mind up and running again.

Two days later, Mora stormed into Philippe's hotel room. He'd just picked up Wolf's trail. One of his contacts in Brussels had seen him walk into a café that was a regular haunt for a small neo-Nazi group. But they'd have to act fast: he likely wouldn't be in town for long.

Mora asked Philippe if he wanted to come with him. Philippe wasn't sure. A manhunt, he thought. That's what Mora was proposing. Tracking a bloodthirsty animal into a corner. He knew perfectly well what Mora was thinking, he knew the hope that swelled his heart. He knew because he could feel it, too. He had only to think of Laurent and the desire for revenge would surge through him. A call for blood. So, yes, he did want to hunt down the animal and take it out.

He told Mora he'd be with him for as long as it took. He wrote a short note to Madeleine, a masterpiece of things left unsaid: "I'm out of the country with Mora for a few weeks to meet some people, I'll be in touch, I love you, etc. etc." He hastily moved his things into Olivier and Marie's old apartment then he jumped on a train with Mora.

And the hunt began.

In Brussels, the bird had already flown. Thanks to Mora's contact there, they found one of Wolf's men. They had a free and frank exchange of views, at the end of which a new destination was on their radar.

They took another train.

Antwerp, Rotterdam.

Again they were too late. They kicked in doors and twisted arms. They heard this and that. They got wind of an attack in another city. And they were off again on Wolf's trail, not quite sure if they were chasing a man of flesh and blood or no more than a ghost.

They travelled the length and breadth of Europe. The clatter of train wheels against the tracks and the rumble of locomotives resonated all the way into their bones. They took tunnels and bridges, walked through deserted train stations in the dead of the night, and crossed fields that all looked the same in the middle of the afternoon.

Soon they hardly spoke to each other. They were reduced to shadows that walked, sat, breathed, and slept side by side, barely aware of each other.

Cologne, Bonn, Frankfurt, Heidelberg, Stuttgart. Everywhere the same scenario: meetings in squalid cafés; brief discussions in hushed tones with jumpy, worried individuals; trying their best to bring their point across in English, French, and German; warm beer and bitter coffee; greasy sausages knocked back on the run; seedy hotel rooms infested with vermin. Then the train again: the uncomfortable seats and the countryside streaming by in indistinct lines outside the windows.

Wolf sometimes left behind more tangible tracks: ransacked apartments, tortured bodies. And everywhere the police lazily treating each incident as an isolated case of racist violence, failing to join up the dots to other, similar cases. By crossing border after border, Wolf managed to put some distance between his actions, his misdeeds disappearing into the "news in brief" sections, settling at the bottom of the eighth page of the final section of the newspapers, somewhere between the deaths and the horoscopes.

Mora and Philippe were like sleepwalkers. Haunted and exhausted, they forged on, voiceless behind the screen of smoke from their cigarettes. The times, dates, and cities, their arrivals and departures, they all melted into a shapeless jumble. Their undertaking was nothing more than a never-ending race, every movement and destination running away from them like a fistful of sand.

Munich, Salzburg, Vienna. Prague, behind the Iron Curtain. Then at last, after five months of frenzied marauding, Berlin. They'd reached the end of the line.

Chapter 19

Lanaudière, October 2002

"We like to think our parents will go on forever, don't we? We imagine we'll have time to catch up on all the moments we lost, we'll find a way to smooth out our differences and tell them we love them. But my parents disappeared overnight, without warning. It was a phone call from the States at dawn that told me they were dead. Brutally murdered in an Ohio motel. No motive, the local authorities thought. They never were able to find the guilty party.

I didn't get it. What the hell were they doing in Ohio? Why were they killed? It's not true what I told you: my parents weren't Nazi hunters. They would meet up with lots of people and constantly be on the move from one place to the next, sometimes even in South America. They never told me why. Truth is, they never told me a thing. Our family was all secrets and reading between the lines. A blind respect for authority, only adults were allowed to talk, corporal punishment as soon as you stepped out of line: that was my education. There was a reason I left home as soon as I could.

Nothing explained why my parents had been murdered. So I tried to find out. I moved into their house and started rummaging around. From one wall to the next, one storey at a time. I gathered up every scrap of paper I could lay my hands on, including what they kept in two safety-deposit boxes at the bank, and hidden away behind a dummy wall in the basement.

The first thing I noticed was that there wasn't a word about them before they came to Montreal. No documents, no passports, no photos. As though they hadn't existed before 1950. Or had reduced their own history to nothing. After throwing away everything of no interest, I split the rest into two piles.

The first contained newspaper cuttings going back over 20 years. They were all about ex-Nazis being hunted in such and such a country for war crimes: about them being discovered, arrested, then running away. I didn't understand why they'd collected all that. Were they planning on writing a book? Hoping to recognize people they used to know who hadn't been locked up? I had no idea.

The second pile left me even more confused. Notebooks filled with names and addresses, with links to other names and addresses, and accounting ledgers full of international money transfers. I didn't get it. Huge amounts of money had been moved around over the years. Why had they sent all those people money?

I was none the wiser for weeks, then I received a visit from a man who said he was an FBI agent who had investigated my parents. I wanted to know more, of course, and asked him to come inside. What he told me was their real story.

My father's name wasn't Yakob Moranowitz, but Hörst Fuller. He was in the Nazi Party, the SS, and the Gestapo. He'd gone to Paris at the same time as the German army. Had played a part in the Gestapo's abuses in France. Had met a young French girl by the name of Paulette Dubois, who was charged with collaborating with the enemy after the Liberation. My father had been sent to Yugoslavia in 1943, then to Poland as a guard at the Chełmno extermination camp, in February 1944. When the camp closed in January 1945, with Soviet troops approaching, all trace of him was lost.

It wasn't until recently that the FBI agent had found my parents, who, now married, were called Morane. Both had belonged to a network where ex-Nazis would help each other out. It had been active for 20 years or so in North America. The FBI had been about to arrest them when they were murdered. The agent suspected they'd been killed by members of a group known as the Bundle. It was a relatively small but very violent neo-Nazi group, led by an individual known as Hank Walsh, no doubt of German origin, who had probably left the United States and crawled back into the woodwork.

The FBI agent asked me if I happened to have any documents that might be able to help him with his enquiries.

It was a terrible shock. I'd always thought of myself as a Quebecer of Jewish-Polish extraction, the grandson of victims of Treblinka, and I'd just found out that I was the son of a French collaborator and a fucking Nazi who was being hunted for war crimes! I gave the agent all the documents I'd gathered and showed him the door. I was drunk for days.

I got paid a second visit one week later. A man calling himself Hans Wolf knocked on my door, pointing a revolver at my gut and asking for a few minutes of my precious time. He had a story for me about my father, too. It turned out to be a good bit more detailed than the FBI agent's.

My father, Hörst Fuller, was born in Kiel in 1911. His own father had been a baker and a corporal in the artillery in the First World War. My father had grown up poor, and times had been tough after the war. Every summer, he'd been sent as a youth to a well-off cousin of his mother's in Alsace. There he'd learned French, fallen in love with France, and discovered Paris, promising himself he'd return one day.

He passed his exam to become a mechanic in 1930, but since Germany was in crisis, he hadn't been able to find work. He would hang around with the wrong crowd, get into fights, and get involved in little schemes. One of the guys in the wrong crowd was called Kurt Wolf. It was Wolf who convinced him to join the Nazi Party in 1930 and then in 1931 the SA, the *Sturmabteilung*, the famous Brownshirts. Things didn't get any better than that for two out of work hoodlums who were chomping at the bit for a little action. They left the SA before the Nazis cleaned things up, and both signed up to the SS in January 1933. Right before the elections that would bring Hitler to power.

Back then, most of the SS were no more than volunteers, but the organization was often used as a recruitment centre by its members. From late 1933, Wolf got an SS friend to do him a favour and he got into the Gestapo, the brand new secret state police force Göring had set up in Berlin. As for my father, after a spell as a mechanic, then a truck driver, he was unemployed again. Wolf did him a favour in turn, and my father was able to become police auxiliary for the Gestapo. He gradually began to make a name for himself. He became a *Kriminalangestellte*, a desk job, in 1937 and *Kriminalassistant* in early 1939, tasked with following up on the files of French nationals in Germany. By then he was an SS-*Unterscharführer*, a sergeant. His French no doubt helped him get the job.

That same mastery of French explains how he found himself in June 1940 as part of the special commando force for the Reich Security Main Office that set up in Paris on the German army's coattails. My father's immediate superior was the SS commander Karl Bömelburg, who was head of the Gestapo in France until late 1943.

There's no way to tell what my father got up to in Paris, but he seems to have enjoyed his time there and gone to plenty of parties. The French section of the Gestapo carried out all kinds of atrocities against the Jews, members of the Resistance, and communists. It can be supposed that my father took part in that kind of thing without too many reservations. In any case, it was in Paris that he met Paulette Dubois, who became his mistress.

He was unceremoniously recalled to Berlin in March 1943. He'd been caught using the black market, or maybe accepting bribes? No way to tell. The only thing for sure, is that it was serious enough for him to be demoted from sub-lieutenant to sergeant, back to where he'd been when the war started. Then he was sent to serve as a guard at the Chełmno extermination camp in Poland.

Surprise, surprise, there he found himself reunited with his old pal Wolf, who'd been there for a while. But deporting Jews to the camp had just stopped, and they were getting ready to close the place. Less than a month later, Wolf and my father, accompanied by 83 others who worked at Chełmno and their commander, captain and police commissioner Hans Bothmann, were dispatched to Yugoslavia to shore up a military police unit attached to the 7th SS-Division Prinz Eugen.

Until this point, there might be reason to think, or at least hope, that Wolf and my father were nothing but a pair of moderately enthusiastic police officers who did no more than obey orders. That was definitely no longer the case in Yugoslavia. As well as fighting against Tito's communist Partisans, they also retaliated against civilians suspected of supporting the Resistance. Wolf showed me photos from back then. I destroyed them a long time ago, but I'll never forget them.

There's a Serb in one of them, face down on the ground. His head is in a pool of blood while an SS celebrates over him. In another, a man has been crucified with pitchforks against a barn door. Rape scenes. Little girls, old women, it didn't seem to make a difference. Men decapitated with axes. Hangings by the dozen. Barns set ablaze with men, women, children, babies trapped inside. An entire village burned to the ground. The worst was the one I recognized my father in: rifle in hand, he'd just bayoneted a pregnant woman.

In February 1944, with the Jewish ghetto of Łódź—the last ghetto back then in Poland—set to be liquidated, the Germans decided to reinstate operations at Chełmno, and Hans Bothmann and his men were called back to Poland. They built two barracks and two cremation pits. The victims arrived by train or truck, and slept in the church. The morning after they got there, they were taken to the barracks to undress. Then they crammed them into a truck, gassed them, and burned the bodies. Seven thousand people were killed like that in June and July, 1944. Wolf drove the truck that took the Jews from the church to the barracks. My father drove the one that gassed the Jews.

After that, the Germans decided to send the last survivors from the Łódź ghetto to Auschwitz Birkenau to speed things up. They began dismantling Chełmno and erasing signs of the murders that had been committed. Halfway through December 1944, all the buildings there had been demolished.

The Soviets were coming, and Bothmann and his men were awaiting orders. Those orders never came. Bothmann decided to liquidate the group of forced workers before leaving. Many of the prisoners were given the task. Some burned the bodies and gathered up the ashes. Others were chosen to work with the staff, or for their expertise as carpenters, tailors, shoemakers. Their feet were in chains and they were often executed and replaced by others. By that stage, there were only 47 workers at the camp. During the night of January 17 to 18, the operation got underway: the prisoners were taken in groups of five to the edge of the forest and killed with a bullet to the back of the head.

Wolf and my father were no longer under any illusions about what the future might hold for the Third Reich. And they were too fond of life, apparently, to defend the motherland to the death. So they came up with a plan. They volunteered to escort the prisoners to the barn where they stayed until they were brought to the site where they were killed. They escorted the first two groups without a problem. But the people in the third group threw themselves at them and ran off into the surrounding forest. Wolf and my father quickly came to their senses, opened fire, and chased after them.

One of the prisoners was called Yakob Moranowitz. He was a Polish Jew, the only survivor of a family that had been completely wiped out at Treblinka. Yakob had quickly become a handyman to the SS, washing their clothes, waxing their boots, playing music on an old violin. My father was very fond of Yakob. He was a good worker and very cultured. My father would often have long conversations with him.

Together with Yakob, Wolf and my father had come up with a daring plan: they would open fire on the five prisoners as they ran off, not hitting them, then chase after them. That way, all seven of them would be free. Of course, poor Yakob and his friends didn't know about the second part of the plan. As soon as they met up in the woods, Wolf and my father executed the prisoners without the slightest hesitation. There was no way they were going to desert with five Jews who would give them away the first chance they got. But there was a third part to the plan, and this time it was Wolf who was in the dark. Fuller opened fire one last time. Since Wolf didn't speak Polish, he would have jeopardized the plan, too. My father then swapped clothes—and identities—with Yakob, and hightailed it out of there.

It's something of a miracle that my father managed to escape without getting caught by the Gestapo, the Wehrmacht, the Ukrainian Fascists, or the Polish Partisans. But the fact that he'd learned Polish over the course of countless conversations with Yakob likely helped.

Kurt Wolf survived the wound, but wasn't able to catch up to the SS from Chełmno. They'd already left the camp. Two days after that, the Soviets arrived.

While Wolf headed off to another camp, this time as a prisoner to the Russians, my father managed to cross Poland and make his way to France. He found the woman who had been his mistress in Paris, changed his name again, this time to Jacob Morane, and married my mother. A few years later, smelling trouble—some people who'd witnessed his handiwork in Paris with the Gestapo recognized him—my parents fled to Canada.

Wolf got off lightly, at the end of the day. Captured by the Soviets, he was sent to a camp where the National Committee for a Free Germany came for him, then trained him. Like many ex-Nazi police and security officers, he was recruited by the Russians. The Americans did the same, by the way. Four years later, Wolf started studying radiotelephony and journalism at Karl Marx University in Leipzig, a recruitment pool for the

Hauptverwaltung Aufklärung, the foreign intelligence service of the GDR.

In 1961, following a number of assignments in Eastern Europe, the HVA planted Wolf in West Germany. His mission was to infiltrate and manipulate groups of young people who were craving a little action. In barely a few years, and apparently without any misgivings, Wolf had gone from being a sub-lieutenant with the SS to a communist agent.

He quickly specialized in infiltrating far-right groups, managing to put together a particularly efficient network that organized attacks intended to spread panic and give the impression that neo-Nazis were on the rise across Western Europe. But Kurt Wolf had another objective: getting his hands on my father. He wanted revenge for how my father had betrayed the man who had once been his friend. He picked up his scent in France, but much too late: my parents had long since emigrated. Struck down by a nasty case of cancer, Wolf died in 1968, without being able to carry out his plan.

But his son Hans, who was born in 1950, was already following in his footsteps. From 1972 on, he started playing the same role as his father: infiltrating and manipulating groups of extremists while under the orders of the HVA. He was much more successful than his father ever had been. He founded the Bundle in 1975 and extended its activities all the way to North America. He tracked down my father in Montreal in 1978. That's when the blackmail began: 'You work with me or I turn you in.'

My father wanted to have it both ways: claiming he was prepared to collaborate, while contacting the FBI and trying to negotiate immunity in return for leading them to a dangerous East German spy. A meeting was set up with Wolf at a motel in Ohio, with the FBI all set to come storming in.

But when the police got there, all they found was my parents' bodies. Wolf had killed them long before the meeting was to take place.

Wolf wanted my fathers' papers. I had to tell him I no longer had them. Strangely enough, he didn't seem overly bothered. My father's network, he told me, was nothing more than a bunch of old cripples. It was night and day between it and the network he was putting in place. If he'd taken an interest in my father, it was to kill him. A promise he'd made to his old man.

Trouble was, now that I'd seen him, I'd become a problem. But he had a proposition for me. He'd spotted me when he'd been keeping a close eye on my parents, and had been impressed by my talents as an activist and organizer, by my physical prowess and gift for languages. So he proposed I work with him. If I refused, he'd kill me, too. I had two days to think it over.

I decided to disappear that same night, sneaking over the roof of the business behind my parents' home. I made it downtown, where I rented a room. I organized my escape the next day. In the time it took to empty my parents' bank accounts and put their house up for sale, I was on a plane to Vancouver.

Funny enough, I landed on my feet in Vancouver. I had enough money to keep me going a good while, and would have even more once the house was sold. I began studying Nazism, fascism, and the far right. I wanted to understand how people could subscribe to such hateful ways of thinking.

I threw myself into my work to stop thinking about my own situation. It didn't help. The more time passed, the more empty and disgusted I felt, torn between feeling angry or depressed. It wasn't until I began reading up on the children of Nazis that I realized I was far from unique.

Everyone who'd found themselves in that situation—discovering the crimes of their parents and having to deal with their denials and their silence—had a hard time coping. They became haunted by a past that wasn't their own. Sometimes they even wanted to shoulder the blame for their parents' crimes, inheriting a guilt that their parents had probably never felt. Even though the dates of birth of the children of Nazis immediately absolved them of all responsibility, they couldn't help but wonder what they would have done had they been in their parents' shoes.

I told myself I had two options. I could either become the exact opposite of my father, like so many other kids in Germany who got involved in left-wing terrorism. Or I could take on the role of the son of a Jew who died in a camp. I could reincarnate myself as the son of the real Moranowitz, and I could avenge him. Getting revenge for Moranowitz meant killing Wolf and, indirectly, my own father. That second option seemed to be the only chance I had of giving any meaning back to my life.

First off, I had to find Wolf. I reached out to experts, historians, security buffs, terrorism specialists. I met with the FBI agent who'd visited me in Montreal. He put me in touch with others, who put me in touch with others, and so on. Gradually I was able to build a network that was solid financially and logistically, a network that aimed to bring the fight to the extreme right, the Bundle in particular, and Hans Wolf most of all. I took on the name Moranowitz, and from that moment on, I hunted down Wolf like my life depended on it."

Mora fell silent and brought the cup of tea to his mouth. It was the first time he'd touched it since starting his story.

A long silence settled down over the cabin, as Philippe fought the anger that was growing inside him.

"Why did you lie to me all this time?"

"Would you have helped if I'd told you I was the son of a Nazi?"

"Maybe. I don't know."

"Would you have helped if I'd told you I was the son of a Nazi who was going after another son of a Nazi who was manipulating a far-right network as a communist agent in the West?"

"I doubt it, no."

"That's exactly what I thought back then. And then one lie led to another, and there was no way I could reveal the truth."

Philippe grumbled in disgust, but he had one last question.

"How come Wolf picked up where he'd left off when he came out of prison? The wall had come down, there was no East Germany anymore. It didn't make sense any longer, did it?"

"Maybe he really does believe in the superiority of the Aryan race? Or maybe he's been out of control for a while now, even under his old bosses? I honestly don't know. What I do know is that without the ex-GDR spy service at his disposal, he would only have managed to put together a small group. Capable of doing damage, yes, but nothing like what we went up against back in the day."

"I see."

"What do you want to do now?"

"I don't know," Philippe shot back. "I'll have to think it over."

Philippe stood up and walked past Mora without giving him a look. He took two cigarettes and a lighter from Christian, picked up his coat, and flounced outside.

Mora remained motionless, his eyes lowered and his arms folded. Two minutes later, he went back into his room.

Christian let himself fall back into his chair. Out of habit, he turned to look at the screen. Against all odds, there was movement. A red SUV was slowly making its way along the slope that led to the cabin.

He jumped up so quickly that he knocked the chair to the floor.

"Robert! Come have a look, quick! They're moving!"

Chapter 20

Berlin, June 1987

Philippe had lost all notion of time. He couldn't have said how many days he'd been in Berlin for. As though suddenly nothing was important. He was nothing but a tourist, wandering through a city he didn't know, with no points of reference. A tourist who was now lost in his own life.

Every morning, he'd wake up in his neat and tidy room, then have a quick wash before going downstairs for breakfast. As soon as his meal was over, he'd set out in search of adventure, with no other goal in mind other than to explore, discover, and stroll around. He'd only go into a café to have a beer and get something to eat, usually alone, or read a book.

Mora had requisitioned a table at the back. He would set himself up there in the late afternoon, then spend the rest of the day there. He'd become unbearable. Mora now had a thick jet-black beard that gave him the off-putting look of a persistent offender, while Philippe had shaved his off. Lots of people shuffled over to Mora's table. Who they were, how they knew him, and why they came to see him, if not to be chewed over and spat out, Philippe had no idea. Mora spoke German more often than not, and much of the conversations would go over Philippe's head.

That afternoon, Philippe was sitting less than five metres away from Mora, who hadn't noticed him, occupied as he was berating one of his informants, a gummy-eyed, haggard-looking boy with long, greasy hair.

"*Mein Gott!* Are you kidding me? You think I give you all that money to hear garbage like that? *Alles Scheiße! De la merde, tout ça!* Don't forget, *mein Freund*, that if it wasn't for me you'd still be strumming your guitar in a dive bar for a few *Pfennigs*. So figure it out and find something *schnell* dammit!"

And the informant would run off with his tail between his legs, while Mora cursed the poor bums with nothing better to do than spend their days hanging around Berlin.

"*Schluss! Schluss jetzt!*" he shouted, pounding his fist on the table.

A string of swear words followed in three languages, and Mora pored over his papers, reading through reports and newspaper cuttings while muttering incomprehensibly to himself.

Philippe wondered, as he had every day since coming to Berlin, what exactly he was doing there. Why didn't he just drop it, leave Mora's whining behind, forget all about wandering the endless streets of the foreign city, and go back home? But "back home" had never seemed so abstract to him. He was no longer at home in Montreal, and he never really had been in Paris. In Berlin, he was nothing more than a ghost prowling around in limbo. Where on earth should he go next? And what should he do there? Now and again, he would think of Madeleine. His picture of her was becoming less clear by the day, less and less real. Sometimes he would doubt that she even existed, telling himself that she might have been dreamed up by a delirious mind.

He'd written to her, of course. Ten postcards in five months. Sent from just as many European capitals and absolutely inane. He had no idea if they'd reached her, and even less of an idea of her state of mind when she might have read them. He hadn't sent one since reaching Berlin. What could he have written? Weather is lovely, wish you were here?

The carousel turned every day: endless wandering; interrogations; despair, anger, and resignation. In Berlin, they say, everything moves slowly, but he felt listless more than anything, repeating the same movements again and again, thinking the same thoughts that inevitably brought him back to square one. Not a day went by without thinking of Laurent, too. Then his anger would flare, giving him the energy he needed to put off his thoughts of leaving until the next day. If only Mora could find a lead. If only something would happen and they could get it over with.

Fortunately, there was Ingrid. A tall, broad-shouldered blonde with high cheekbones and sea-blue eyes, always even-tempered. That very instant, she was bringing him over a greasy *Weisswurst* with fries and a pint of stout. She set it down in front of him and began to talk.

Unlike many Germans, Ingrid enjoyed chatting with strangers. With foreigners—*Ausländer*—especially. Even though Philippe was no longer a stranger, she still enjoyed talking to him. Her English was crystal clear, and she could manage a few words in French, delivered with an accent he would happily have called exotic, all with a smile that never left her lips.

The first time Philippe had set foot in the café, accompanied by tight-lipped and sullen Mora, he'd apologized for the sand they'd dragged in with them on their shoes, left over from a construction site they'd just traipsed through. In Berlin, Ingrid had taught him, a little digging and you hit sand right away. "A little sand isn't the end of the world. Sand is fluid and eternal, just like Berlin!"

She'd grimaced the morning he'd told her he was off to see the wall. "No one mentions the wall here. It's there, it will still be there tomorrow and the day after, so why worry about it? It's best to talk about other things."

He'd gone to see it just the same, of course. He'd taken Straße des 17. Juni, which cut through the *Tiergarten*, leaving a large gap between the trees, and kept on walking until he hit the wall. *Die Mauer*. The "Wall of Shame" or the "Anti-Fascist Protection Rampart"? That depended on your point of view.

Philippe had been very surprised to discover that you could just walk up to it. You could even touch it. He could have climbed up on it, but there was nothing to see on the other side, nothing but a no man's land with, a little further away, another wall. Right in the middle, all at sea, stood the Brandenburg Gate, Berlin's own Arc de Triomphe, topped by a carriage and four horses.

To his mind, he should have found himself on the brink. As though there had been on that very spot the abyss left behind by a sphere that had been split in two. On the one side: us. On the other: them. Half the world looking at the other through warped glass.

The emotion he had felt at first had quickly dissipated. It was nothing but an ordinary wall, made from concrete blocks with a tubular top. It wasn't especially high. It was dirty and covered with blue, black, red, canary yellow, and luminous green graffiti. With political slogans, obscenities, and bad jokes. With giant penises and stylized bodies, stupidity and subtlety, hyperrealism and expressionism. Like a misleading advertisement, a façade that had been put up to host a gallery.

The following day, Philippe had hurried over to the East. He took the *S-Bahn*, the downtown railway, to Friedrichstraße station, where there was a crossing point. After an interminable wait to go over the border, he reached

Unter den Linden, the magnificent avenue that had once been the heart of the city. There were crowds, just like in any major city, but they wore strange clothes and shoes that seemed to come from another time. Trabants in impossible colours—powder blue, lemon yellow, concrete grey, apple green—spluttered their way along the streets. He passed by a long string of embassies, poorly stocked store windows, drab and dusty bookstores, tall and imposing buildings. In the strip running down the centre of the avenue, Frederick the Great sat aside his charger. Two identical cathedrals stood in one of the side streets: the *Deutscher Dom* and the *Französischer Dom*. One only just renovated, the other in ruins, as though the bombs had fallen the day before. A plaque at Bebelplatz recalled the book burning of 1933: "On this site, Nazi barbarism destroyed the finest works of German and world literature." Philippe then crossed the Spree and strolled around the Museum Island, drawn in by a half-collapsed wall, its beauty as magical as the ruins of Ireland. Then he crossed the second branch of the Spree and ended up at Alexanderplatz, a huge square surrounded by a series of 1950's apartment buildings. He spent hours in the narrow streets, among buildings that dated back to the start of the century, the odd remaining graze, scratch, and scrape left behind by machine-gun fire, bomb explosions, and shrapnel. No matter how clichéd it sounded, that hadn't stopped it crossing his mind: it was as though the armistice had been signed only the day before.

But just as Ingrid had said, it had all quickly faded away. Once he'd touched the wall and crossed over to the other side, Philippe hadn't thought of it again.

"*Guten Appetit!*" Ingrid said to Philippe, who was alone with his sausage and beer. The only sound in the café came from the discreet clinks of the knives and forks of the other customers, and from Mora's grunts as he listened to another informer report back to him.

Philippe leaned down over his plate, but Mora appeared in front of him, excited, incapable of stringing two sentences together without every other word being in German.

"Calm down, would you? Take a deep breath and tell me all that again slowly."

"I've found Wolf!"

Mora had tears in his eyes as he clasped Philippe in his arms, forcefully enough to crack his bones. In a split second, Philippe had his friend back.

Philippe was sauntering along, more and more pedestrians coming to join him on the sidewalk as he advanced. At a bend in the road, a side entrance appeared in the *Tiergarten* fence. Two police officers were politely and discreetly checking bags, controlling the entrance to the park.

The people waiting in line in front of Philippe showed no surprise, concern, or impatience, as though there was nothing at all out of the ordinary. Maybe it had always been like that, he thought. Maybe in Berlin there was a police checkpoint for every crowd. He'd seen a lot of police the day before along the Ku'dam, heavy machine guns on their backs. That night, police cars had raced down Kurfürstenstraße, sirens blaring, escorting a convoy of a dozen military vehicles. The police were planning for the worst. But maybe that was to be expected in Berlin. After all, just like Ingrid had explained to him, barely a month and a half earlier a riot had broken out in Kreuzberg, a poor neighbourhood that was home to Turkish immigrants, students looking for somewhere cheap to live, squatters, punks, anarchists, and leftists of all stripes. There was a street festival at Lausitzer Platz every May 1. The police, that one time, had decided to move in and break up the crowd. Perhaps to push back against the *Schwarzer Block*, or the "Black Bloc" as the press called them, anti-establishment protestors who dressed in black and covered their faces to avoid being identified by the police. Wading indiscriminately into the crowd, the police set off a chain reaction. Protestors reacted by throwing stones, glass bottles, and Molotov cocktails until the police, beaten and humiliated, were driven out of the neighbourhood. Looting followed, and a supermarket was burned down. "See?" Ingrid had added, giving him her air-hostess smile. "Now *that's* Berlin."

A police officer went through Philippe's bag and sent him on his way. He headed to Straße des 17. Juni. The broad boulevard ran the length of the *Tiergarten* and was perfect for a military parade. That's where the growing crowd was going. There was another police checkpoint to be negotiated on the way, though. Two minutes later, Philippe was standing by the street.

Waist-height metal barriers separated the sidewalk from the road. The smell of beer and fries hung in the air, as children ran around shouting and megaphones crackled incomprehensibly in German, English, and French.

Everything was in place. The crowd seemed to be ready. The only thing missing was the parade. For the time of day, the 17. Juni was deserted, aside from a handful of police officers pacing around in riot gear, visors under one arm. To Philippe's left, the metal bridge of the *S-Bahn* cut across the street and curious onlookers had already positioned themselves on it. To his right, he could see the temporary seating platforms that had been put up just for the occasion, most of them still empty for the time being. It would clearly be a while before the parade got underway. Philippe decided to use the time he had to get something to eat. He moved away from the crowd and walked in under the trees.

A hundred metres or so further on, he sat down on an empty bench. He produced a can of beer and a large sandwich from his backpack. He was just about to take a bite when a shadow passed in front of him. Mora sat down on the bench, too, stretching out his long legs in front of him.

"Hey Philippe. Not just early, but thinking ahead, too! May I?"

He took the can.

"Hi Mora. Be my guest."

"It's hot out today. You'd think it was summer. Cheers!"

Mora knocked back a generous slug of beer.

"Ah, that hit the spot," he added, wiping his mouth with the back of his hand. "What do you think of all this, then?"

"I dunno. I find it all a bit strange. What's the parade in honour of?"

"Are you serious? You must be the only person within a 50-kilometre radius who doesn't know!"

"Come on. I only speak two or three words of German. Are you going to explain it to me or not?"

"It's the 'Day of German Unity.' June 17."

"German Unity? Berlin is celebrating German unity with a parade of American, English, and French troops? Am I missing something? And why June 17?"

"Philippe, you're a lost cause. It's to commemorate June 17, 1953. Stalin had just died, but the East Germans were hell-bent on being more Stalinist than the Soviets. When the authorities increased work quotas, the construction workers went on strike. The strike spread, leading to protests, until finally the people took to the streets. The Soviets stepped in, of course. They declared martial law and, on June 17, 1953, quashed the uprising. In the West, they made June 17 a public holiday, the Day of German Unity, and ever since they've organized a parade to show that no one's forgotten."

Philippe nodded as he took a bite from his sandwich.

"Okay. So Hans Wolf wants to use the occasion to make it clear what he personally thinks of the foreign armed forces in Berlin, is that it?"

"That's what I think. That's what my informant says, at least."

"And what if he's wrong? Or he's stringing us along?"

"Then we'll have wasted a day."

Philippe sighed and picked up his beer.

"I don't see what Wolf could have planned."

"Maybe he thinks now's the time for a little action, time for some collective hysteria, you know? But as to how? I don't know any more than you do."

"Your plan?"

"Keep an eye out around the street and try to spot Wolf or his men."

"None of this is sounding very professional."

"I know. I think it's been a while since we were professional. Any better suggestions?"

"Warn the police?"

"You tip off the police that there's gonna be a terrorist attack and you'll spend hours, if not days, trying to explain how you know. You feel like doing that?"

"Not really, no."

Mora took the beer out of Philippe's hand. The sandwich was finished.

"If you ask me," Mora went on, "if Wolf decides to make an entrance, it'll be from the *S-Bahn* bridge—because it'll be spectacular and he'll have armies parading just below—or from the platforms for the officials. Or somewhere in between. Or both."

"How can he hope to do a thing? There are police and dogs everywhere. And they probably went over the route this morning."

"I know. That's Wolf's job, pulling things off even though the police are around. That's what he specializes in. I don't know what else to tell you. We're going fishing. I'll take the *S-Bahn* and you find someplace between the bridge and the platforms, okay?"

"Okay, but I'm not feeling it. I'm not feeling it at all."

"We'll see."

Mora stood up and disappeared into the crowd. Philippe swallowed the little bit of beer that was still sloshing around at the bottom of his can, then stood up and headed back toward Juni.

The crowd was much thicker than the first time around, and the stirrings were shriller, more sustained. The time was coming, the tension was rising. Philippe decided to go have a look at the platforms for the officials. He followed a path that seemed to lead there, but it quickly veered away from the road and into dense undergrowth. Two rows of barbed wire had been rolled out in the bushes, barring his way. A police officer stood in his path. *Verboten*. Philippe turned back.

He found himself in the same place as before, with three rows of people standing between him and the metal barriers. There was a side street just in front of him. An ambulance was parked on it, two ambulance technicians pacing up and down beside it. The *S-Bahn* bridge rose up to his left. Among the crowd gathered up near the bridge, he caught sight of Mora's long aquiline nose. Mora motioned discreetly to him. He was wearing binoculars around his neck and regularly scanning the street and the crowd with them. To Philippe's right, the VIP platforms were slowly filling with stiff, austere bodies.

There was nothing to do but wait. Wait and keep an eye on the people around him, the kids being hoisted up onto shoulders, the sausages and buns being wolfed down, the plastic glasses of beer being lifted to mouths. Watch the nonchalant police officers who passed the time stomping around, facing the crowd, foreheads pearling with sweat. Look up to the helicopters circling over the park. Hear, but pay no attention to, the nonsense coming out of the loudspeakers. Nothing to do but rock back and forth on his heels, put his hands on his back or in his pockets, scratch an ear, his chin, the top of his head. Nothing to do but keep his eyes peeled, scan the crowd in search of a sign, a clue, something that looked off, someone acting strangely.

He wondered what Wolf might be trying to do. Blow up the *S-Bahn* bridge? Who knew how that might end. Set off a bomb in the crowd and sow panic? Why on earth would Wolf do such a thing? Even though he seemed to have no qualms about murdering people, he tended to kill clearly identified targets. Maybe he'd attack the armed forces, then? That might make more sense, but it would be hard to organize. Might he attack the VIPs? They were foreign military and politicians. Yeah, Philippe thought. If I were Wolf, that's what I'd try to do: plant a bomb on the VIP platform.

Philippe turned to face the VIP area. Lots of people were sitting there now. High-ranking officials and local politicians, by the look of things. Quite the target. How would Wolf get to them? No doubt he hadn't been able to plant a bomb before the parade: the police had been over the area with a fine tooth comb. Maybe he would strike from a distance, with a rocket launcher? It was hard to imagine him getting close enough with a weapon like that, using it, then hoping to get away. A suicide attack? That couldn't be ruled out, but it wasn't really the Bundle's style.

Philippe looked carefully at the people around him. What would a bomber look like? Not like anyone around him, he thought. But who was he to know? He sighed and shook his head.

A murmur rose from the crowd and the agitation grew around him. The crowd closed ranks, the loudspeakers became even more vehement, and as though responding to an invisible signal, the police officers donned their masks as one, adjusted their chin protectors, and turned to face the crowd.

The first platoons paraded by. First came the brass bands, the musicians marching in step, eyes trained on their scores, representatives from each army group filing past. The crowd was treated to the usual feats of military prowess, batons hurled high into the air, knees left exposed beneath Scottish kilts. Then came the infantry, parading in close order. Tough customers all, red in the neck and closely shaven under their gleaming helmets, feet striking the ground to the same beat.

Shouts rang out. Jeers and the odd insult. Philippe turned around. A dozen people were standing behind him, most of them young. A few looked like they were straight out of the 1960s (bushy beards, John Lennon glasses, flowery dresses), while others were dressed as punks (studded leather jackets, green and orange mohawks). They shared the same loudmouthed enthusiasm.

"Noodles!"

The soldiers couldn't possibly not hear them, Philippe thought, but they didn't so much as flinch. They kept on marching, impassive, eyes expressionless, limbs stiff. The protest seemed to be no more than a handful of individuals, armed with nothing more than their vocal cords. No sign of a bomber or anyone sinister-looking. Mora looked down from high up on his bridge, shrugging his shoulders to show there was nothing he could do.

Philippe turned around again to see that a police cordon had been put up behind the protestors, hemming them into a semicircle that he was right in the middle of. And those police officers, unlike the ones who had been baking for hours out on the road, had a glint in their eye and their muscles at the ready.

Philippe realized that the slightest misstep would leave him trapped between the crowd and the barriers, unable to lift a finger. He inched slowly to his right, treading a delicate path until he moved beyond the police cordon. What he'd lost in peripheral vision—the low-lying trees now prevented him from seeing the platforms—he'd made up for in potential mobility. Mora approved his move with a nod, but was again forced to give him another shrug. Nothing, *nichts*, *rien*.

The jeeps backfired as they arrived, pennants waving in the wind, followed by cannons and, the highlight of the show, the tanks. The smaller ones first, as though to temper expectations, then the bigger ones. Monsters, Philippe thought to himself, as the machines of apocalyptic proportions advanced down the road, accompanied by the squeaks and squeals of their tracks on the tar. Plumes of black smoke rose into the air, and the ground shuddered beneath his feet.

The five U.S. tanks that passed by Philippe screeched to a halt and the din died down. There were shouts to his left. The police spoke briefly into their microphones. The shouts drew closer, and the police officers moved swiftly in their direction. A young woman was racing down the middle of the road on her bicycle, weaving between the stopped tanks. Brandishing a clenched fist in the air, she hurled insults that Philippe assumed were directed against the military. The soldiers remained stony-faced in their vehicles, but the police tried to stop her. She managed to avoid a few of them, but then one got hold of her sweater. He made enough contact to knock her off balance and she toppled into two police officers. They seized her by the waist and she struggled furiously, kicking and screaming. Apart from a few bursts of applause, most of the crowd just smiled or shook their heads. The protestor calmed down eventually, and the police took her behind the barricades, where other officers were waiting.

Amused by the performance, Philippe looked up to the *S-Bahn* bridge. He saw Mora in a panic, hopping up and down and waving like a lunatic, gesturing toward the platform. Philippe looked behind him, but the trees were obstructing his view. He motioned to Mora that he couldn't see. Mora lifted his arm and brought a hand up in line with his nose. Then he put his hand on the top of his head, moving it around in a circular motion. Lastly, he traced a rectangle around himself, from his shoulders to his knees.

Okay, Philippe thought to himself. A man of medium height on the platform, short or cropped hair, wearing a cap and a raincoat. He nodded and Mora disappeared back into the crowd. The tank closest to him revved its engine with a dull roar that shook the crowd to its core. Philippe turned toward the tank. The soldier manning the turret remained expressionless. The diesel engine rumbled again, but it was immediately drowned out by the tank's gun going off.

It was as though he'd just been struck by lightning. Philippe found himself on the ground, in a free-for-all of strangers' limbs, his head between a man's knees and his nose flat against the grass. Nothing moved, and the absolute silence lasted for an eternity—maybe half a second. The very next instant, everything around him was transformed into a single shriek that left thousands of mouths at once, a furious stampede, a crush of feet, elbows, and fists thrown blindly, children crying, bodies stepped over or trampled on, shredded clothes. He freed himself from the hysterical tide as best he could, coming to rest against the barrier that stood between him and the road. He gave himself a quick once-over and, finding himself still in one piece, looked up at the tank. All things considered, the shot hadn't come from that one. The soldier posted at the machine gun on the turret was bent double, hands over his ears, looking over his shoulder in horror.

The platform, Philippe thought. Of course. A bomb had just gone off on the platform, right behind the trees. He saw a column of thick, black smoke, heard the roar of the flames, and, over the shouts of the crowd, could make out cries of absolute terror, shouts of impossible pain.

The crowd had quickly moved away from the scene of the explosion, and Philippe was easily able to move in on it. He was looking for someone who looked guilty and was running away. But all he saw was a shifting mass of men, women, and children, pouring out of the park's paths in a foaming torrent. And, going against the flow, a handful of police officers and firefighters, trying to reach the platforms.

Philippe continued to look for the man Mora had described, someone of average build, with a shaved head or short hair, wearing a cap and a raincoat.

A siren sounded in the distance, followed by another. Soldiers cried out, garbled orders came from all sides, and again there was the rumbling of engines and the creaking of tank tracks.

At last, he saw him. Hands buried in the pockets of a midnight blue raincoat, wearing a military cap, a man was sauntering away from the site of the explosion. A smile spread itself across Philippe's face. He set off in pursuit of the man, quickly reducing the distance between them. When he was only 50 metres behind him, he slowed down to walk at his pace.

Walking into the café, Philippe saw Mora at once, sitting at one of the tables at the back. Empty glasses of beer stood in front of him. He looked riled. He had the face of a man who'd lost, of a man who always backs the wrong horse, not realizing it until he returns home, his pockets empty. But Philippe was wearing the grin of a man who'd just won the lot, after backing an old nag at 50 to 1. Mora noticed and froze, his features locked in fearful expectation.

Philippe motioned to Ingrid for two pints of stout.

"So?" Mora finally asked, his voice husky, when Philippe sat down in front of him.

"*Guten Abend!*" Philippe replied.

Mora muttered something that was barely inaudible.

"So?" he said again, sounding impatient.

"Ah! Our beers. *Danke schön*, Ingrid."

Mora rubbed his eyes, trying hard to be patient. Philippe picked up his glass and took a long drink.

"Ah, that's nice! Walking so long out in the sun makes a man thirsty."

He sat down his glass and wiped the corners of his mouth with the tip of his fingers. Mora was going through torture.

"So, now that I think about it…" Philippe began again.

Mora raised an eyebrow. Philippe took another sip of his beer.

"You know the guy with the short hair, who was wearing a military cap and coat? You know the one I mean?"

Mora nodded mechanically.

"Well, I followed him."

A grin spread across Philippe's face.

"And I have an address!"

Chapter 21

Lanaudière, October 2002

Philippe plodded along the road. The air was cold and damp, but the exercise kept him warm. The road hugged the lakefront, and occasionally the water could be seen between the tree branches. The cabins were rare and deserted, their occupants having abandoned them to the approaching furies of winter. A stellar silence reigned around him; it seemed as though the forest had swallowed its every sound. There were no birds in the trees, no chipmunks darting among the dead leaves. Barely a rustle from the bare branches when the wind picked up. The silence was broken only by the regular sound of his feet striking the ground.

His anger subsided as he walked, but he felt as though he'd been had. The story he'd just heard was too over the top. Mora, the son of a Nazi out for redemption? And claiming that killing Wolf was the way to achieve that? It was hard to swallow. But at the same time, why on earth would Mora come up with such an unlikely scenario? He had nothing to gain from it, quite the opposite. It had to be true. So the part about being the son of a Nazi was okay then. But Philippe's own involvement in the story didn't come out of it looking too good. How naive he'd been to let himself be manipulated like that. Philippe recalled the well-meaning pretensions of the young man he once was: he'd been out to change the world. Based on that presumption, Mora had seemed like a good man to follow.

If he'd known his real identity, Philippe wondered, would that have changed a thing? Doubtless it would have in Paris, when they'd first met. He would have sent the Nazi's son packing without a second's hesitation. In Berlin, he wasn't so sure. He hadn't really been tagging along behind Mora, by that point. He'd followed him across Europe for one reason alone: revenge. Even now, memories of Laurent would leave him seething inside.

But that was just the thing: he was no longer 25. He was no longer the young man who allowed anger and hatred to cloud his judgment, or at least he hoped he wasn't. So what was he doing, then, striding along this sandy track, turning over dark thoughts in his mind, when he could be at home nice and warm, with his wife and kids? What a poor excuse for a father he was. Judging by his own behaviour, it was hard to resent Mora for lying and hedging his bets. Philippe felt like a real idiot, a complete moron. It was as though he hadn't learned a thing over all those years. He was still repeating the same mistakes, destroying the only things that were ultimately of any importance to him.

It had to stop. But how? As he walked, everything that had seemed clear to him an instant before fell apart and slipped through his fingers. The more he thought about it, the more doubts he had about getting the police involved. He knew how good Wolf was at slipping away to be under any illusions. Even though he was older now and had seen better days, he could still easily escape. The slightest doubt, the slightest suspicious sound, and he'd be gone without a trace.

And though it pained Philippe to admit it, part of him— far from the most admirable part—was chomping at the bit to set fire to the cabin and gun down everyone inside.

There was no denying how powerful and invincible he'd felt when he'd touched the assault rifle. The very same second he'd picked it up, he'd realized how easily everything could go off the rails. All it took was a weapon, a death to be avenged, and the very worst could happen. Mora knew exactly what he was doing by giving him the gun. It was the ultimate temptation. Philippe hated him for catching him out like that, and he hated himself even more for considering the option. Despite how tired he was, despite the wear and tear of past years, he had to admit that he still had enough rage inside to empty every magazine he had.

But he wouldn't do it. Not any longer. He promised himself that much.

What should he do, then? For the moment, walk and clear his head. Then talk some sense into Mora, call the police, and head home. What did he care what happened after that? It was no longer his fight.

He looked at his watch and realized he'd been walking for an hour. He felt as though he could have walked all the way to Montreal, as though he could have kept going until he dropped with exhaustion, but he turned around. No point getting everyone worried on top of everything else, he thought. He began to walk back the way he'd come, looking around for a pebble to kick.

Three pebbles had disappeared off the side of the road when he heard an engine. The information slowly worked its way into his mind. An engine. A car was coming. He turned around. Behind him, the road sloped gently for around two hundred metres before breaking off at a right angle to the left. He waited in disbelief as the sound of the engine grew louder and the crunch of the tires on the sandy track became clearer. A car hood appeared at the bottom of the curve, a star-studded reflection.

Philippe dived into the ditch. Branches whipped his face, stones ripped into his sides, and cold, damp leaves wound up in his collar. He buried himself in the leaves and rolled over, his head barely raised. A car was crawling along the road, a red four-wheel drive with oversize tires, its engine snarling as it inched up the incline. He saw four people through the windows before the car disappeared.

Heart pounding, he picked himself up and walked on.

He had been walking for an hour. He'd covered four, five kilometres.

The car would be there in less than five minutes.

His lungs were on fire. He tried to keep a hold on the panic that was taking over his body, driving him on. He couldn't run any faster; he'd used up all the strength he had. A hill stretched out before him. He was sweating. His pulse was beating in his ears like a drum, but on he went. He had to get there before the car did; he had to. The cabin was behind the trees, less than a hundred metres away, he was sure of it. He stopped and tried to catch his breath while he listened. Nothing. Not a sound. Without a second's hesitation, he cut off through the trees. His feet caught and he stumbled. He fought back the branches that were conspiring against him.

Every three strides, he stopped to listen. Silence—still—surrounded him, and he could hear nothing but his heart hammering in his chest. He plowed on, trying to go as fast as he could while making the least amount of noise.

At last, between the tree trunks and the branches, he caught sight of the sloped roof with its black asphalt shingles and wooden panelling. A little further on, parked right beside where Mora's car was hidden, the red four-by-four he'd met earlier. Philippe took a few more steps, more careful than ever. The closer he got, the more worried he was. He stopped at the edge of the wood and lay down in the damp leaves, barely covered by the bare trees. At last he heard a sound. There was a commotion. Chairs were knocked over.

A bang.

Two seconds went by, then a second bang.

Philippe stood up, ready to run in and attack. He wasn't carrying a thing, not so much as a pocketknife. Nothing but two empty hands and a bellyful of rage against four people who were armed. He considered going around to the other side of the cabin, rolling under the boat for the gun. But before he could even take a step, another commotion rocked the cabin and the back door was flung open. He scrambled back in among the leaves, hiding himself as best he could behind a birch tree.

A man came out and ran over to the four-by-four. Philippe didn't get a good look at him, but he was fairly sure it was Cowboy. He started the engine, turned the car around, then backed up to the little log staircase that led up to the cabin. He stopped, leaving the engine idling.

Through the bare windows, Philippe could see only shadows moving around inside. There was only one thing he could do: sprint over to the lake, dart around the three birch trees, cut back to the cedar hedge in front of the cabin, then get to the boat. On the count of three, he thought to himself. Now or never. At that very moment, the cabin's back door opened again and Philippe dropped back down into the dead leaves.

Mr. Muscle and someone Philippe didn't recognize came out through the door, made their way down the steps to the parking space, and got in the car. The fourth man came out of the cabin at last. A sturdily built silhouette in a dark raincoat.

Philippe recognized him. Hatred washed over him, and he fought back the urge to wring the man's neck.

Wolf closed the cabin door and walked calmly over to the stairs. He stopped when he got to the top. He raised his nose and sniffed the air, wheeling around. His eyes shifted to where Philippe was hiding and Philippe was sure Wolf had sensed he was there. For five long seconds, Wolf kept his eyes trained in his direction, while Philippe could only hold his breath.

Wolf turned around and went back to the four-by-four. Philippe buried his face in the dead leaves, stifling a cry of rage. He heard the car door slam, then the car drove off.

It wasn't until he lifted his head again that the smell hit him.

The smell of burning.

Chapter 22

Berlin, June 1987

Philippe and Mora forced open the barricaded door of an abandoned building in the Kreuzberg neighbourhood. They set themselves up on the top floor of the building, with sleeping bags, blankets, water, and all the provisions they needed to squat there. The broad soot-smeared windows gave them a fine view of the building that Philippe had found.

It was on the other side of a parking lot that contained three derelict delivery trucks. The one-storey brick building stood at the far end, carved open by three long, horizontal windows. The windows were black as ink; the place seemed to be empty.

All they had to do was wait until someone showed up. Hours passed. Mora, posted by the window, binoculars in hand, staked out the building while keeping a distracted eye on the clamour of the city, the rumbling of the trucks going down the street and the higher-pitched cars. Philippe, sitting in a corner, was trying to read, nibbling without conviction on a bland sandwich, before giving himself up to fitful sleep in his too-thin sleeping bag. He and Mora swapped shifts regularly. A thrum was all around them, a form of torture apparently destined to drive them both out of their minds: Turkish music playing in the background, stopping at nightfall only to pick up again at dawn. They sighed, cleared their throats, coughed, cursed softly to themselves, muttered jokes that fell flat. Time passed a little more.

They'd been inside the abandoned factory for 48 hours. Mora was snoring heavily in his sleeping bag. Philippe had squeezed himself into the corner of a high window whose pane was shattered. He glanced down at his watch. Seven minutes past ten. Ever since the sun had set, the damp had cut right through them. Nothing was happening down below. He set down his binoculars and adjusted his coat collar again around his neck, barely able to contain the involuntary motion of his jaws.

What was the point in waiting for so long? Not the slightest thing had happened. But he was sure he wasn't mistaken. It was definitely that door the man had gone through after Philippe had followed him through the streets of Berlin. Maybe he'd followed the wrong person? Or maybe the man had realized he was being tailed and had led Philippe back to what was nothing more than an abandoned warehouse? Perhaps Wolf had already fled West Berlin? Perhaps he'd gone back to Paris once his dirty work was done?

The whole thing was ridiculous. That place was ridiculous. Racing around Europe was ridiculous. Ridiculous and absolutely useless. Pathetic, he thought to himself. That's what they were: pathetic. They hadn't stopped a thing, they'd been no help at all. They'd formed a sorry, grotesque double act; Mora thinking he was out to save all humanity, and Philippe, naively running along behind him.

It wasn't going to work, he could feel it. Nothing would happen. And he was fed up. Fed up with being on the losing side. Fed up with the damp that chilled him to the bones, with being thoroughly uncomfortable, with the plaster dust that lined his nostrils, with the smell of mould and urine that made him feel sick. Fed up with day after day bringing nothing but a little more emptiness inside him, leaving him a little rougher around the edges, a little more depressed. And, somewhere above it all, he was fed up with the desire for revenge that was eating away at his soul.

He looked at his watch again. Nine minutes past ten. He shivered and rubbed his hands together.

Fair enough, Philippe thought to himself. He gave himself one more night. Until eight o'clock the following morning. After that he was done, *fini*, *kaputt*. Whatever happened, whatever Mora might say, it was Game Over and he was drawing a line under the whole business. Others could go around Nazi hunting. He'd given enough. He was out. He'd go back to Paris, finish his thesis, then fly home to Montreal and try to make up with Madeleine.

He promised himself that much: tomorrow morning, eight o'clock. Not a minute longer.

He picked up the binoculars and scanned the base of the building, happy at last to have made his mind up. He left the binoculars trained on his target, not believing his eyes. He adjusted the focus, but he was forced to admit the obvious.

"Get up, Mora! There's movement below. Three people just pulled up on motorbikes at the main entrance. And Wolf's there."

Mora jumped to his feet, instantly awake. He snatched the binoculars out of Philippe's hands and peered out the window.

"I see two motorbikes. They didn't even bother hiding them. Three of them went in, you say?"

"Uh-huh. Two men in jeans and leather jackets. One was the man I followed here. The third was Wolf."

"You're sure it was him?"

"Trust me. I'm not gonna forget that guy's face in a hurry."

"Oh… they're moving again. All three have just come back outside. Wait, what are they doing? Yeah, you're right. That *is* Wolf with them."

Mora was shaking with emotion. The grimy abandoned building suddenly seemed charged with electricity.

"He's giving orders to the other two. They're nodding. They're putting on their helmets and getting on their bikes. Wait, no… Wolf isn't putting on a helmet. What's he doing? He's not going with them. The other two are going."

Even from up on the sixth floor, the shrill blast from the powerful Japanese engines could be heard. The motorbikes roared off and disappeared into the night.

"They're gone. I don't believe it. Wolf's stayed behind. He's gone inside. He's in there, all by himself."

Mora lowered his binoculars.

"We're going down and we're sorting this out. Right now. If it all goes to hell, we each go our own way and meet at the café tomorrow morning, eight o'clock. Let's go!"

As though in a dream, his body numb and his mind in slow motion, Philippe watched Mora turn around, take something out of a backpack, stand up, then run off to the stairs. He felt his own body begin to move, his legs activate, the breath move into his throat, the blood pound at his temples.

Less than two minutes later, they were walking through the entrance to the parking lot. They sprinted over to the wrecked trucks, then to the building. They crouched down with their backs against the brick wall, hidden between two rusty oil barrels, out of breath and ears pricked. The silence was absolute, save for a faint strain of music that slipped out from inside the building, accompanied by a husky woman's voice and its inimitable tremolo: "*Non, je ne regrette rien…*" The asshole is listening to Édith Piaf, Philippe realized in disbelief. Just over their heads, one of the rectangular windows had been pushed open. Mora leaned over to Philippe and whispered into his ear.

"Give me a boost up to the window."

"Are you crazy?"

Mora pressed a finger to his lips and scowled.

"Not so loud! Now's no time to get caught. Once I have a hold of the window frame, make plenty of noise."

"What kind of noise?"

Mora tutted with impatience.

"How should I know? Make a noise. Something that sounds normal, loud enough for him to go to the door to see what's going on."

"Okay, okay, I'll come up with something."

"As soon as he moves, I'll sneak inside."

A heavy silence ensued.

"What then?"

Mora gave him a worrying smile.

"Then? I take care of our problem. Once and for all."

He lifted up the edge of his sweatshirt to reveal the dark blue glint of an automatic weapon.

"Shit, Mora. You're not serious?"

"Do I look like I'm joking?"

They stared at each other for a moment, then Philippe shook his head.

Mora put his hand back up his sweater.

"Here. This one's for you. Just in case."

Philippe felt the cold metal in his hand.

"Remember to take the safety off and put the bullet in the chamber, eh? Otherwise there's not much point in carrying one."

Philippe nodded. Mora took the pistol. He pressed the gun to his abdomen and stifled the click as he locked and loaded it.

He tucked the gun into his belt, behind his back. Philippe did the same, although he didn't cock his.

"You gonna be okay?" Mora whispered.

There was a brief silence while Philippe tried to swallow his saliva. His mouth was as rough as sandpaper.

"Yeah, I'll be okay," he nodded at last.

Mora put his hand on his shoulder.

"You're the only guy I can really count on. That's what people call friends, I think."

He tightened his grip, his fingers digging into Philippe's flesh.

"Right, let's go."

Philippe put one hand on top of the other and Mora stepped onto them. Philippe winced: Mora weighed more than two hundred pounds. He pushed up with his legs and Mora, after a wave of his arms, was able to lean on the window frame. He turned to Philippe and, with a nod of the head, gave the signal.

Philippe took two deep breaths. After checking that his gun was still on his belt, he picked up an empty garbage can. He sneaked along the brick wall without making a sound. Once he reached the corner of the building, he raised the garbage can over his head and hurled it into the middle of the parking lot that belonged to the gas station behind the building. The can crashed to the ground, bouncing and rolling around. Philippe hunkered down against the building, his eyes glued to the steel door.

The music stopped. Seconds later, a rectangle of yellow light stretched across the parking lot. Philippe backed into the shadows. He had time to see Mora slip inside the window like an insect scurrying into a crack in the floor. Philippe didn't move, barely daring to breathe. Interminable seconds ticked by. The yellow rectangle grew smaller, then disappeared, and the door clicked shut. Philippe scanned the parking lot. No one. He made his way back the way he'd come and hugged the wall once he reached the window that Mora had disappeared through. A heavy silence reigned inside the building. Suddenly the lights went out.

Muscles taut, Philippe didn't allow himself to breathe. He was wondering if he should try to make it inside through the window as well when he heard the roar of the two motorcycles.

Things were still quiet inside the warehouse. The noise of the motorbikes grew louder still as they pulled into the parking lot. Their headlights fell on the garbage cans, oil barrels, and other junk that was in front of Philippe. The engines were turned off. From where Philippe was hiding, he could only see the front wheel and half the frame of one of the bikes. He reached nervously into his sweater. His hand gripped the gun and flicked back the safety and armed it. He saw a man in a helmet walk around the bike, silhouetted against the streetlight.

Two shots rang out inside. The man beside the motorbike shouted. The door was flung open and clanged against the brick wall. There were shouts, shadows ran around, then two more shots rang out. Philippe stood up and pointed his gun at the silhouette ahead of him. The man crouched down behind the motorbike, holding up what seemed to be a weapon. Philippe aimed for the helmet, and his finger pressed down hard on the trigger.

An incredible explosion went off right at that moment. Philippe toppled forward and rolled between the garbage cans and the junk.

When he picked himself up, a thick column of black smoke was escaping from the window. He shook his head. He was safe. He'd lost sight of his gun. He didn't know if he'd fired. But where his target had been standing an instant before, he now saw a man kneeling down to help another man on the ground. He was holding him by the collar, trying to rouse him. The man let go after a few seconds and got on his bike. He started the engine, glanced over at the window that was spouting black smoke, and slowly drove the motorbike toward Philippe. Philippe was searching frantically for something to stop him with when his eyes landed on a beam.

As the biker gunned the engine and began to accelerate, Philippe jumped up and swung the beam in his direction. The force of the impact hurled Philippe back against the wall. He blacked out.

The noise was deafening. A forge clawed at his ears, its breath scalding his neck. Dazed, he opened his eyes and closed them again, trying to gather his wits. It was night. Glowing red lights danced at the windows of the building across the street. He was slumped in a pile of debris, his sweater snagged against a rough brick wall. He looked up to see a long, open window from which there emerged a thick plume of black smoke.

A dull thud sounded behind him, a powerful explosion followed by the crystal-clear tinkle of shattering glass. A hail of shards rained down onto him, a shower of burning confetti. The window above him was gone, blown out by the explosion. A tongue of fire slipped through the opening and licked at the brick wall, towering high into the sky as it gave off acrid smoke that reeked of gasoline and melted rubber. A look of panic crossed his face as he struggled to stand up. He put his weight on his left arm, but pain shot through his shoulder. He dropped back to the ground. Slivers of glass bit into his cheek. The heat was infernal. The smoke thickened around him, and he began to choke. He rubbed his eyelids, coughed hard enough to bring up a lung, and in one despairing effort tried to pick himself back up, taking care to protect his left arm. Amid the rubble, he managed to bring himself to his knees. He felt a warm, sticky liquid on his hands. They were covered with blood.

Shrill police sirens began to echo in the distance. Philippe moved away from the wall and straddled the biker. The man was lying on his back, motionless. Philippe turned back toward the burning building. He took a step closer to the warehouse, but stopped right away, unable to bear the intense heat it was giving off. There's nothing I can do, he thought. No way to get inside. He'd lost Mora.

Out of the corner of his eye, Philippe saw the biker stir. He lifted a knee, and the helmet shifted on his head. In a sudden, desperate rage, his thoughts turned to Mora who was now burning to a crisp inside the warehouse, to Laurent, to the victims of the bomb at the military parade, and to all the others. Philippe picked up the first thing that came to hand, a long lead pipe, and brought it down onto the biker's throat like an axe.

He began to run.

Chapter 23

Lanaudière, October 2002

Darkness had set in beneath the damp branches of the fir trees in the undergrowth. The rain had stopped and the sky was starting to clear. The moon was rising, coming out from behind strips of torn clouds to light up the tips of the trees with a ghostly glow.

Philippe sat shivering in Mora's car. Everything was saturated in a pungent burned odour, and a thick mass of smoke was swirling over the remnants of the cabin. All that was left of it was a pile of charred beams and red-hot firebrands.

Philippe had walked around the burning cabin and seen that the back door was intact. He'd kicked it in and taken a few steps inside, but the draft of air had only stirred up the fire even more. The heat from the blaze was unbearable, and the smoke was so dense that he practically couldn't see a thing. Nothing but shadow and shimmering ripples, flames everywhere. Eyes watering, he'd had to go back outside. He'd scrambled up the steep slope that led to the parking space and had taken refuge in the car, only able to look on as the inferno performed its sorry spectacle. By some miracle, the fire hadn't reached the surrounding forest.

An hour later, the structure had come clattering down in a shower of sparks. Freezing rain had begun to fall.

A quick search of the car had given Philippe a few supplies: granola bars, some fruit, water. And a half bottle of rye. He brought the bottle to his mouth for regular sips, barely enough to moisten his throat.

A demented giggle crossed his lips, the first stirrings of drunkenness.

Maybe it wasn't a good idea to start drinking, he thought to himself. Even in small doses. But it was probably best to be a little drunk if he was to go through with what he was about to do.

Another giggle escaped from his throat, and he permitted himself another sip of rye. When it came down to it, he couldn't have cared less if he managed to pull it off or not. What would success mean anyway? Avenging his friends' death? Putting a dangerous criminal out of commission? Or just getting his conscience to stop howling? It made no sense. Even once he was dead and buried, Wolf would be replaced by another, younger, psychopath, who was perhaps even crazier and more dangerous. Besides, soothing his conscience was a lost cause. He couldn't even get Berlin out of his head. It was probably best not to set the bar too high.

Berlin. The police and firefighters' sirens blared from all directions. Philippe had had to leave Mora behind in the burning warehouse. Replay over and over again in his mind the image of his own finger pulling the gun's trigger, his hands bringing the lead pipe down onto the motorcyclist.

He hadn't dared go back to his room. He'd hidden in a small park from where he could watch the outside of the café and the door leading up to where he slept. Nothing moved. The street was deserted.

His hopes of seeing Mora reappear faded with every passing hour as dawn approached. The café's metal shutters had opened, the first customers had gone inside. Ten o'clock, and still no sign of life from Mora. Having lost all hope, Philippe had headed back out with the troubling sensation that he was being followed. He'd gone out of his way time and time again. He'd run down side streets, doubled back on himself, ducked into a doorway, collar up, head down, then sprinted over to a taxi. He'd left the taxi, taken a bus, gotten off two stops later, then ran some more. Exhausted and in a panic, he'd booked a room in a small hotel.

He could have sworn they were looking for him. There was a price on his head. He left his hotel in the middle of the night and hurried to the station. Took a train to Hamburg. Then another to Paris, where he found a room in a seedy hotel next to the Gare du Nord. There he'd called one person after the next. Had tried every number he knew, and other numbers when he didn't even know who they belonged to. Drop-off points, people to call in an emergency. In Paris, in the provinces, then further afield. Brussels, Amsterdam, Bonn, Munich, London. Nothing. Tumbleweed. No answer. "The number you have dialed is not in service."

Alone.

He was well and truly alone.

There was no network any longer. There was nothing left. Anyone who had belonged to it was dead, had disappeared, or was lying low.

So Philippe decided to put an end to it. He used the debit card Mora had given him to pay for his hotel and buy a plane ticket to Montreal. He wrote a long letter to Madeleine, telling her everything, all about his adventures and how helpless and confused he felt. About how he felt scared and had run away. About how he felt ashamed and full of regret. Before hailing a taxi to the airport.

Fifteen years later, Philippe realized that he'd abandoned Madeleine again. He'd let her down for principles that now seemed unjustifiable to him, loathsome even. He'd slipped away like a thief, presuming that once again she'd forgive and forget. But she'd never forgive him turning his back on her this time. He wished he could go back, but it was too late. Too late to fix it, straighten things out, get her to forgive him.

Today he'd let Mora down a second time. And this time he was well and truly dead. Just like Christian. Two more deaths. Anger suddenly overwhelmed him, intense and absolute, like he hadn't felt in years. The type of anger that sends a man off the rails, that demands action.

Another swig of rye. The alcohol didn't burn his lips or his throat. The sign that it was time to swing into action. He glanced at his watch, but the light from the moon wasn't enough to tell the time by. It had been dark for a long time. That's all he needed to know. He left the car, walked back down the slope, and worked his way around the smoking ruins of the cabin until he reached the overturned boat on its blocks. After groping around in the dark, he found the assault rifle that Mora had hidden under the seat along with its magazines. He slipped them into the broad pockets of his coat. There was an old shed behind the boat, its worm-eaten wooden walls no longer straight. He kicked open the lock. He rummaged around but couldn't find a glass bottle. Though he did find an almost full ten-litre jerrycan of gasoline.

Philippe moved to the water's edge. The lake's surface was an impenetrable black, smooth as a mirror. Across the bay, all the lights at Wolf's lair were out, except for a small floodlight by the side door that lit up part of the grounds. The bare trees cast long shadows in the wan moonlight. It all made for a bleak scene, but it suited Philippe's intentions down to the ground. He slung the M4 over his shoulder and picked up the jerrycan.

He was getting ready to make his way back around the cabin when something caught his attention at the far right of his field of vision and got him to turn his head. A boot was sticking out from the cedar hedge in front of the cabin. He stood there for a moment, stunned, but quickly gathered his thoughts. He ran over and grabbed hold of the man who was lying under the hedge. He yanked him closer and rolled him onto his back. Christian. Covered in burns, blood running down the back of his neck. His eyes were closed and his mouth was open. He looked every inch a dead man. Philippe suddenly flew into a panic and felt Christian's neck for a pulse then, bringing his face to his mouth, tried to detect a breath.

He was breathing. Feebly, but he was breathing.

Christian was still alive. He could be saved. But he would have to act quickly.

Philippe swore, cursing all the time he'd wasted. He threw away the assault rifle and took the magazines out of his pocket. He put Christian over his shoulder and walked over to the car. He propped Christian up as best he could in the passenger seat then got in beside him.

The key was in the ignition. He started the engine and put the car into reverse, the sand squealing in protest beneath the wheels.

Chapter 24

Montreal, July 2003

Philippe is sitting at the kitchen table with the Saturday newspaper and a second cup of coffee. He's trying to take an interest in current affairs, but it's not working. He can only look. For signs, for clues.

He tells himself he should stop following the news. But he can't help himself, even though he's aware just how senseless his mission is. It's been like this for years now: for every terror attack, big or small, Philippe wonders who's behind it, if it might be Wolf lurking in the shadows, pulling the strings.

He doesn't know, and no doubt it's better that way.

What he does know is that he doesn't want to hear another bomb or bullet, the roar of the flames, the cries of pain. He's had enough of the hatred and the deaths. But he also knows that the memories of those fires will never leave him. They'll be with him right up to the very end.

Philippe pushes the newspaper away and finishes his coffee. The wooden table is scratched and surrounded by mismatched chairs. Nothing matches in his apartment. The walls are bare, there are still unpacked boxes in every room. He's like a young student moving into his first place.

Lucas is playing on the computer in the spare bedroom. Dominic is bored to tears in the living room, waiting for his brother to come back. But Lucas doesn't want to, so Dominic snipes at him until his older brother shouts back and tells Dominic to leave him alone.

Philippe thinks he should have brought them to the park and let them burn off a little energy. But he didn't feel up to it. Anyway, there goes the doorbell already.

Dominic and Lucas shout "Mom! Mom!" and rush to be first to the door. Philippe gets up and goes over to join everyone in the hallway.

The boys are already in their mother's arms, prattling away about everything that happened that week.

"Calm down, boys. Calm down. Let your mom get her breath back, would you? Go get your things."

Philippe finds himself face to face with Madeleine. They peck each other on the cheek, make small talk. He notices her new hairdo—it really sets off her eyes—and tells her it looks nice. She's all smiles, radiant. Happy, even. It's a punch to the gut for Philippe, even though he forces himself to grin.

The boys come running back, carrying their bags. More shouting and pushing. Philippe tells Madeleine to have a good day, tells the kids to have a nice week.

Madeleine and Dominic are already heading to the car, but Lucas hangs back in the doorway. He lifts his head and gives his father the most honest look.

"Dad… Why don't you come back home? Things were good before."

Philippe sighs and bends down, his face in line with his son's.

"It's not that simple, eh? Mommy and I still love each other, but not like before. I'll explain it to you one day, but it's better like this for everyone. Trust me."

Yeah, he thinks to himself. One day I'll have to explain to the kids that when two people stop trusting each other, they can't get it back. And that it was his fault, of course. It was all his fault.

Lucas nods, even though his eyes go cloudy.

"And it doesn't change a thing between us two, right?" Philippe asks.

The boy thinks for a moment, still staring at his dad.

"No, it doesn't change anything. But still…" He shrugs. "That's life!"

Philippe gives him a hug, then ruffles his hair as he gets back to his feet, even though he knows Lucas hates that.

"Go on. Don't make your mom wait."

Lucas flashes him one last smile before racing off.

More often than not it's at night, when he can't fall asleep, alone in his cold bed, that the faces of the past come back to him. He can't help but think back to them. And he can't help but feel guilty. He knows there's no getting away from it: those memories will stay with him until he breathes his last.

Sometimes he also imagines what his life might have been like, if he and Madeleine had stayed together. The scenes play out, each better than the last, but the happiness quickly fades.

So his thoughts turn to the future. To his boys, to the lives they have ahead of them, lives that they'll face—he hopes—calmly and confidently. Things are fine, Philippe thinks. Things are fine.

At last, he falls asleep.

Firebrands

Firebrands
A NOVEL

MARC MÉNARD

Translated by **PETER McCAMBRIDGE**

Original version published in French as *Brasiers* by Les Éditions Somme, 2021.
Copyright © 2021 by Marc Ménard, Tête première.
Copyright © 2022 by Peter McCambridge for the English translation.

All rights reserved. No part of this book may be reproduced, for any reason or by any means, without permission in writing from the publisher.

Copyediting: Jennifer McMorran
Author photo: Claude Barbeau
Cover image: Greg Rakozy (Unsplash)
Cover design: Leila Marshy, Debbie Geltner
Book design: DiTech

Library and Archives Canada Cataloguing in Publication

Title: Firebrands : a novel / Marc Ménard ; translated from the French by Peter McCambridge.
Other titles: Brasiers. English
Names: Ménard, Marc, 1960- author. | McCambridge, Peter, 1979- translator.
Description: Translation of: Brasiers.
Identifiers: Canadiana (print) 20210335890 | Canadiana (ebook) 20210335904 | ISBN 9781773901053 (softcover) | ISBN 9781773901060 (EPUB) | ISBN 9781773901077 (PDF)
Classification: LCC PS8576.E534 B7313 2022 | DDC C843/.6—dc23

Printed and bound in Canada

Legal deposit – Library and Archives Canada and Bibliothèque et Archives nationales du Québec, 2022

The publisher gratefully acknowledges the support of the Government of Canada through the Canada Council for the Arts and the Canada Book Fund. We acknowledge the financial support of the Government of Canada through the National Translation Program for Book Publishing, an initiative of the Action Plan for Official Languages – 2018-2023: Investing in Our Future, for our translation activities.

We are grateful to the Government of Quebec through the Société du développement culturel and the Programme de credit d'impôt pour l'édition de livres—Gestion SODEC.

Linda Leith Publishing
Montreal
www.lindaleith.com

"Most people deceive themselves with a pair of faiths: they believe in *eternal memory* (of people, things, deeds, nations) and in *redressability* (of deeds, mistakes, sins, wrongs). Both are false faiths. In reality the opposite is true: everything will be forgotten and nothing will be redressed."

Milan Kundera
The Joke

"The world is a cancer eating itself away."

Henry Miller
Tropic of Cancer

Chapter 1

Montreal, October 2002

Two days from now, Philippe thought, I'll be 40.

He'd dreaded it for the longest time. The date had always seemed so permanent, so definitive. Like the summit of a mountain you'd looked at your whole life, a far-off destination you knew was inevitable but were still in no rush to get to. And once you reached the top, if your ticket was still good, you only got to go down the other side, following the twists and turns of a path long like a tired snake, lower and lower.

Philippe's still-thick hair was barely starting to be flecked by white. His abdomen had a give to it that, 20 years earlier, his flat, hard stomach hadn't known, but he hadn't yet resorted to hiding it under shapeless sweaters. He hadn't smoked in more than a year, kept his drinking reasonable, jogged three times a week, and regularly hit the weights. But there was no getting around it: in two days, he'd be 40.

He sighed.

The young boy at his side looked up and held out his hand with a smile. Philippe took the little hand in his and gave it a squeeze. The light turned green, and they crossed the street. Once they were in the schoolyard, Philippe squatted down next to his son Dominic. In under two minutes, the bell would ring and the children would line up outside the door. He looked around for Lucas, his older son, among the crowd of kids as they shouted and ran around. He found him pretty much right away, hanging from the monkey bars, feet dangling into the void. Their eyes met briefly, and he flashed him a furtive smile that Lucas returned just as discreetly. He was barely ten, Philippe thought, and Lucas was already distancing himself, as though ashamed at the thought his friends might catch him smiling over at his dad.

Philippe turned back to his younger son, fixed the collar on his windbreaker, and planted a noisy kiss on his cheek. Dominic gave him a smile that alone made the trip worth it. Philippe stood back up and watched with his hands in his pockets as his son walked off, backpack and lunchbox slung over his shoulder, swaying beneath the load. The bell rang. The shouts around him grew louder, and the children began to converge on the school. Philippe sighed again and began the walk back home.

The Friday morning was cool for October. The sky was a blindingly clear azure, a sure sign of the last throes of summer. As always, the heavy traffic had ground to an impatient standstill on Henri-Bourassa. He crossed the boulevard, and the blare of the traffic quickly faded, replaced by the leaves rustling in the wind, the warbling of the starlings, and the squirrels scampering through the maples. The canopy formed by the double row of trees made for a protective screen that more often than not left Philippe feeling calm and collected.

But not today. Today the canopy was gloomy and left him with the same suffocating sensation as the too-low ceiling of a damp cave, the walls of the houses around him cold and smooth as death row. He made a face as he neared home, depressed at the thought of starting his workday. Especially since what was waiting on his desk was a long-winded, sleep-inducing treatise on the perils of globalization, which he was to read and report on for the small publishing house he regularly freelanced for. Almost 40 and still having to take on